HAL JOHNSON

Sudden Glory

First published by Spontaneous Combustion Publications
2023

First edition

ISBN: 979-8-9887778-0-9

Cover art by C.G. Coleman

This book was professionally typeset on Reedsy.
Find out more at reedsy.com

For S.J. Archer

·"Dear reader: I know you're reading this..."

Unlike most of my books, this one is not for young readers. If you are under the age of sixteen, or perhaps more plausibly twenty-three, and you find yourself reading this book, please set it down and pick up a different one, perhaps one written by me. If you choose to continue reading this book, please do not get caught. If you do get caught, tell whoever caught you that I told you to put the book down, which, to be fair, I did.

If you are an adult human, perhaps you should put this book down as well. All I can say is that this is a book about 2003, and writing about 2003 with the standards of twenty years after would be in some sense dishonest. Also, the book is 100%autobiographical, except in the sense that almost every incident in it is literally impossible, and therefore didn't happen.

But you know what I mean, right? I hope you, at least, know what I mean.

1

Book I: The Minor Orcana

A diabolical reveller in vices of which he was innocent...
  −Shaw, on Beardsley

· 1 · A few words of introduction · A beginning to all things · Unimportant details about background objects · Our hero, and the love interest · Bathroom time · Why does he have a gun anyway? ·

Green churchmouse ire box.

But that's hardly important now. What's important is that a Saturday dinner at the future in-laws' was wrapping up, and Oscar Cox sat there in the dinette with his napkin on his lap, his messenger bag uncharacteristically slung across the back of his chair. Inside the bag, well-swaddled in tissue paper and a supermarket circular, was the gun the Union had given him.

Oscar tried to act nonchalant.

The Kuntis' house was in Jersey City, up in the Heights. They'd lived there for nearly thirty years—Oscar's fiance had grown up in this little Cape, and everywhere its floors were piled with the detritus of his childhood: the violin case (empty), the ham radio set, the half-completed Lego spaceships. It was all mixed up with the only slightly more faded detritus from V.K.'s older brother and sister, their own ephemeral and forgotten childhood obsessions. And all around, on every pile, were the parents' books: *How to Kill the Klutterbug*; *Simplifying 101*; *Regression Modeling in Actuarial Contexts*; *1969 Dodge Jeep Wagoneer Owner's Manual*; *Cure the Clutter and Free Your X*, where the value of X was concealed by the drooping remains of somebody's 1980s-era science fair project. Those were the titles Oscar could read at the moment, and he was reading them with a wellspring of feigned interest, because every time his mind wandered he found himself clutching his messenger bag.

"Are you okay? What's in the bag? Etc.," everyone asked. And Oscar would let the bag swing away, and say something pleasant and charming about the dinner that concealed the fact that he had forgotten the name of every dish, as well as every ingredient of every dish except for rice.

He could feel the bag pendulum on the back of his chair and he dreaded the moment, inevitable, when Mrs. Kunti would say, "Let me take that for you, hang it up in the closet." Oscar knew the closet was too full of old vinyl and boxes of (perhaps) baby socks to hang a bag in, but it had hooks on the door, so he understood the metonymy of what she meant. What she would mean, that is, were she to say it.

"Look at that thing that is not my bag," Oscar said, only in a more roundabout way. An old, crumbling snap-together model

2

of a Japanese robot atop the cupboard, for example. What was up with that?

"Our boy was always really into that enema stuff," Mr. Kunti explained with the cockiness of an immigrant who was also a native English speaker.

"It's pronounced anime," V.K. said without rancor but immediately, and there was another conversational dead end. The visit could not go on much longer, and yet Oscar was running out of tricks, if by *tricks* we mean *ways of not drawing attention to a messenger bag.*

"Have you read any good books?" he asked the beaming adults, knowing they had not. "Have you watched any prestige television dramas?" Everyone had already expressed sympathy that Oscar's graduate studies were still delayed by a labor dispute; everyone had already gotten maximum mileage out of complimenting Mrs. Kunti's new haircut.

And then, indeed, there was a miracle in the after-dinner silence. Oscar's fiance, V.K. himself, was getting up to go to the bathroom. The half bath with the salmon tile that sat right next to the kitchen.

Oscar knew, and of course everyone knew, what would happen next, the long moment of indecision as V.K. paused in the doorway, his hand already on the inside knob, the door already half shut. Would he shut it the rest of the way?

This was a small drama, but at the very least it was not Oscar Cox's drama. He relaxed his death grip on the messenger bag and watched V.K. stand there. The parents (who must have witnessed this drama more times than Oscar even) watched, too; you couldn't take your eyes away. The door swung three-quarters shut and then hovered, trembling and uncertain. Oh, V.K.! Leaving the door open, with two and an *almost* family members in plain sight at the dinette table would clearly be inexcusable. But closing it all the way, with a terrible click—was this, too, rude? Would he be slamming the door in the face of his loved ones?

Oscar had no problem answering that question, and he would have just shut the damn door, but V.K. would not. But he also would not *not* shut the door—he would not decide that three inches, for example, was the perfect compromise that balanced privacy with companionability. Instead he inched the door back and forth, searching, as he did each time, for the proper ratio.

He erred, unfortunately, on the side of companionability, and so every tinkle and blat, as Oscar sat there with his hands folded, not making eye contact, drifted across the silent, flush-faced table. What were his parents thinking? They used to change his diaper after all; were they not even embarrassed? Three pairs of eyes lingered on the multiple strata of ancient, yellowing paint-with-water papers magneted long ago onto, and never removed from, an invisible refrigerator, its silhouette only implied under the innumerable pages. How strong were those magnets? At least everyone knew the good fellow washed his hands.

And after that, the evening was over, and all was ready for the long drive home. Hugs all around. Thanks and come agains.

"It's really happening, though?" said Mr. Kunti, his eyes dewy with pride. "In one week?"

"As René Magritte said at the construction site," V.K. answered, "this is not a drill."

Needless to say, Mr. and Mrs. Kunti had no idea what their son was talking about. So Oscar quickly dropped some delightful pleasantries that made them love him, that made them forgive their son for getting entangled with someone who 1. was *a.* white and *b.* male and *c.* technically unemployed, in a

4

way; 2. did not love them back; 3. did not even love their son; 4. etc.

The two soi-disant lovebirds headed out into the warm evening and the car, and Mrs. Kunti burst through the front door just as they were pulling away. "Oscar! You forgot your bag!"

The year was 2003, and we were all a lot younger then, and foolisher. Jersey City was crappier. New York City was cheaper and even more cautious than today. V.K. drove—it was his car, and it was his trip as they were his parents—the long way through the tunnel and crosstown congestion and bridge to Queens. He wasn't there yet, though. He was still in Jersey City, on the great slope down to the Hudson, sitting at a four-way stop sign. First one car, then—its headlights a distant will-o'-the-wisp growing closer and larger—another he waved through. Oscar sat patiently, and waited for V.K.'s car to move again, and waited for V.K.

That wasn't his real name, of course, or even his real initials. No one's name is their real name here. All names have been changed to protect the innocent. Therefore, all names have been changed except Oscar Cox's.

· 2 · Some more about our hero · Getting to know you · A series of bad decisions that sounded okay at the time · The veriest varlet · Straighter days · First appearance, old flame · "If it were only the other way!" · The waiting game · Putting the *pan* in *panurge* ·

What a remarkable man is Oscar Cox! What a bulwark, what a pillar! Everything about him is a fake, but it would not do to

5

hate him too soon. He really is rather charming, despite it all.

Lord Macaulay said (of Horace Walpole): "His affectation is so habitual and so universal that it can hardly be called affectation. The affectation is the essence of the man. It pervades all his thoughts and all his expressions. If it were taken away, nothing would be left." But Horace Walpole, to be fair, could not have started out this way. He did not start out affected. How many corridors of shame must he have wandered down, confused, before—if Horace Walpole was anything like Oscar Cox—he hit upon affectation.

If you could have seen Oscar in his heyday—seven, say, years before, ca. 1996—what a bounding Rabelaisian hailfellowwell-met you would have seen! He'd kick down the door of a frat house ten minutes before the party ended, reel across the room while drunks nodded appreciatively at how much drunker he was than they. "Let me tell you—" he would roar, followed by a filthy and only semipossible story of some sexual exploit that had made him late; or possibly of some other party he had come from, at a larger university nearby, one much louder and wilder and freer; but don't feel bad—Oscar had brought a little of that wildness and that freedom, a little of that noise along with him, and here—you could just sip it vicariously from his outstretched palm. This, too was fake, the "other party" and the "triple-jointed coed" and even the drunkenness. Oscar preferred to restrict himself to 0–1.5 beers in any given 24-hour period, so that he could more convincingly ape a shambling, self-destructive trainwreck of a lad. If he got too drunk, he might accidentally do something responsible, or his loose tongue might accidentally let slip words that were about anything other than the endless bacchanal that was his ostensible life.

It's safe to say that only the dimmest and drunkest fratboys believed all of Oscar's yarns, but people tend to subscribe to a smoke/fire theory, and pretty much everyone acknowledged that Oscar was doing *something*, or *someone*, at three in the morning. The correct answer was *problem sets*, but they did not get the correct answer. His last-minute arrivals, his overblown, filthy tales, his careful intimations that he might have a secret double life of crime, had all made Oscar a byword on the campus of A—t College, and to some extent the nearby campi of nearby schools. Had he been seen sneaking out of the dorms of St. Ethel's, the exclusive girls' prep school? Did an exclusive girls' prep school named St. Ethel's even exist? Oh, that Oscar Cox!

He had had a real life, once upon a time. He was a human. He had parents (divorced and remarried). He even had a wicked stepmother, but she was from New England, so it was okay. He has siblings, assorted. Probably someday they should all meet his fiance, but they tended to live all the way in Edgewater, N.J., so it wouldn't be happening soon.

He had had a different fiance, once upon a time, a double-e, acute fiancée, Vera Rodriguez—currently a marine biologist somewhere in some abyssal sea, back then a fellow A—t student and convenient beard (of sorts). When kicking down too many frat house doors at three AM had grown tiring, when the various webs of lies he'd spun had grown too tangled to juggle without accidentally mixing the metaphors, Oscar had very ostentatiously entered into a monogamous relationship. Vera. How difficult (he lamented, after atavistically kicking down a door) to remain faithful, and yet he must! he must! Here he wiped the sweat from his brow, for anything was easier than conjuring up another acrobatic stewardess double-team in the bathroom of a Greyhound bus.

7

Why would airline stewardesses be traveling by Gr—

Quiet, please! Oscar was up all night, when not kicking down doors, reading all he could about sea life, to impress his new girlfriend. But a monogamous relationship posed its own challenges, and Oscar now had to spend his days thinking of reasons not to have sex with Vera. He persuaded her, in direct contravention of all possible evidence that he had ever scattered behind his guilty footsteps, that he wished to wait until marriage. Vera accepted this, but somehow she also accepted it as a proposal. They were engaged for nearly two years, and had even moved to New York together, where they would be attending different but close-enough graduate schools, when Oscar, in some paroxysm of desperation, came out of the closet in order to wriggle free of the arrangement. The breach of promise, but with reasons; these, too, would be fake.

The idea that being a gay man would help you not have sex sounds, in retrospect, so absurd that it demands some defense. It's just that if Oscar's idea of heterosexual behavior had been based mostly on Larry from *Three's Company* and Falstaff, his idea of homosexual behavior had come primarily from reading *The Picture of Dorian Gray*, and it is a bald statement of fact that a close reader could get the impression from *Dorian Gray* that the basest depths of gay depravity are collecting Japanese curios and researching the Italian renaissance.

Nevertheless, Oscar tried. He started kicking down the doors of gay bars five minutes before closing and announcing how many fictional dicks he'd been smoking, but no one found it charming or even odd, so he went back to straight bars, kicked down the doors and milked some glory out of being the token homosexual, who was also an alcoholic and possibly a second-

8

story man, possibly a drug dealer—something shifty about that wonderful Oscar Cox! When this proved tiring, Oscar went monogamous again, and that was V.K. Kunti; fellow New Jersey native, fellow N— Y— University graduate student. With V.K., Oscar insisted that sex would be more special if they waited until they were married, which he thought was particularly cunning because, although once again the scheme ended up with him engaged, two men could scarcely get married in New York in 2003. The burgeoning danger that Massachusetts might sooner or later acknowledge gay marriage, which could perhaps lead a weary fiance to suggest a road trip to nuptials, had a worried Oscar Cox laying the groundwork for the idea that it would be cold-hearted to get married while their brothers in other states (perhaps other countries? Saudi Arabia?) languished in discriminatory celibacy.

W.B. Yeats once admitted that the cult leader Madame Blavatsky was a fraud; "But what is a women of genius," asked Yeats, "to do in the nineteenth century?" Well, what is a man of genius to do? Not that Oscar Cox was a genius, necessarily. He was just really good at math. But what was he to do, regardless? Admit he didn't want to have sex with anyone? Perhaps he could have done that once, had he had more courage, but after a decade of crowing over his outsize libido...it was an awful lot of crow to eat.

And here he was now. Still juggling webs. Four years into a Ph.D. he had not worked on for the last eighteen months. Trapped, as all of us are, by vast impersonal forces we cannot control. His only character flaw, other than an occasional affected tendency to refer to himself in the third person, was the fact that he did not love his fiance. Also, admittedly, he was somewhat dishonest; for example when he said, which he often did to his fiance, "I love you."Or when he said almost anything else about himself.

I hope all possible questions have been answered about Oscar Cox.

Wait a minute! Why does he have a gun in his bag?

What's he supposed to do, leave it under his bed for some toddler to find?

No, I mean, what kind of idiot would give this guy a gun?

Oh. The short answer is a sweaty little man named Mr. Pizzoli. But the longer answer, as is its wont, is longer.

· 3 · A descent to the underworld · Before the law · Feigned competence · The marshmallow exam · We are supposed to be learning how he got the gun, after all · Smoke-free building · Details on the apportionment of departmental funds · A cowardly exit ·

It was the end of July, and the days were getting shorter. The days were long, but they were less long than they had been a month ago, and they were less long each day. Every year starts out, like a life, with promise, with the incremental lengthening of the day, until halfway through it pivots on its summit and begins a long slow slide to night. In its solstitial moment of triumph, day begins to lose, and the story of summer is the story of its loss.

"Days are getting longer," the summer people say to each other, a wicked lie, a denial of the memento mori that tells you *don't get too comfortable leaving for work with the sun overhead; everything will come around to darkness soon.*

Oscar didn't leave for work, of course. But that Saturday

morning, the morning of the day of the dinner, he had left regardless, having been summoned, to see the Union rep. The Union rep was Mr. Pizzoli. This is the origin of the gun.

But you don't just stroll into a Union rep's office and have the power to kill handed to you. First you have to find it, the office, and since it was in a subbasement halfway between the Psych Building and the Nursing Studies Building, this was not going to be easy.

It made no sense as well. At N— Y— University, the T.A.s at the math department (and the geology department) had a different union than the T.A.s of the other departments, and so Mr. Pizzoli, math and geology union rep, represented none of the T.A.s, psych or nursing, whose buildings straddled him. The Math Building (there was no Geo Building) was all the way on the other side of Washington Square.

This—the misplaced office, that is—was hardly unusual, as N— Y— University's so-called campus was a sprawling series of unconnected structures and parts of structures, and it was frequently the case that a math professor, for example, would have his office in the Anthropology Building (which, despite its name, was primarily used for storage and catering) or in a private apartment building or in a warehouse in Brooklyn. The whole thing was a big mess. Even the fetid underground tunnels Oscar was wandering through had never been intended for academic use, but were simply the remains of failed silver mines dug by convicts in colonial days. The ancient graffiti still sported the long ſ, like an integral sign. "Maſter Francis Lovelace, his mother hath a round heel" read one of the few examples not in Dutch.

"Am I even supposed to be in here?" Oscar asked himself, as he pushed through a side door marked *nooduitgang*. And he was not. A woman with a clipboard made that perfectly clear. The sign on her door identified her as Erica Jones, psych. dept., although the general dampness of the air had mildewed into oblivion the first three letters of her name, which caused some confusion. Oscar explained that he was looking for Mr. Pizzoli, and Erica sighed a long theatrical sigh. Her hair, like everyone's, was of a nondescript color, and her eyebrows, while not technically meeting in the middle, were certainly conspiring to meet in the middle. They had dinner plans in the middle, and dinner was coming soon. She was a graduate student, too, and had her own pit to dig for herself, which left little time for Oscar Cox's.

"Pizzoli is right down that hall," she pointed with her chin, "but I'm supposed to check with him before I let anyone through." And that would have to wait, as she had double-booked experiments all day, and (the crazed look in her eyes explained, if she did not) everything would take five times longer than it should and Oscar would never get to see Mr. Pizzoli, and so he would never get home, which was terrible because (you may recall) he was supposed to have dinner at his in-laws in Jersey that night. Clearly she had halted half a dozen applicants and supplicants already today. Clearly nobody saw Mr. Pizzoli.

But this is what Oscar Cox was good at. He was good at looking like he knew what he was doing, a mask that remained ever-fresh, for he had never spoiled it or worn it out by actually knowing what he was doing. "Perhaps you need an assistant," he said. *Departmental funding! Grants don't cover!* But Oscar waved away the objections. He was, after all, a grad student himself and a T.A., albeit one on strike. He was not allowed to do math, of course, *like a dirty scab!* but surely there were no

12

rules against his helping out the psych department. He could administer a few electric shocks to a few test subjects, and we could all be on our way. Had he not taken Psych 101 eight years ago at A—t College? Had he not once read a book by Nietzsche subtitled *Documents of a Psychologist* (1889)?

The wheedling probably (as it tends to) took more time than just checking with Mr. Pizzoli would have, even in a hypothetical subterranean world without phones. But finally it was worked out that Erica Jones would go and look in on Pizzoli, while Oscar held a clipboard and prepared to supervise yet another data point in some replication attempt of the Stanford Marshmallow Experiment.

In case you did not take Psych 101 eight years ago, let us pause to outline what this Stanford Marshmallow Experiment (so-called: We are not in Stanford, remember, and are even some forty miles from Stamford) meant. A child, in this case (subjects are anonymous, but we'll call her) Little Janie, is offered one marshmallow now, with the promise of two marshmallows if she should wait fifteen minutes. A simple test in delayed gratification. Oscar and his clipboard entered a side room.

Of course, Little Janie and her red-faced white-knuckled mother had already been waiting fifteen minutes, or more. The mother had practically gnawed the edge off a tin no-smoking sign. "Let's go, little girl," Oscar said, brightly. He brandished his clipboard so the world would know he was a responsible scientist and not a pervert. As the mother, red-faced and white-knuckled, applied a nicotine patch directly to her soft palate, Oscar clicked the door shut behind him.

Another side room. "Now, little girl," our hero said. They were sitting in tiny chairs that were not comically undersized for one of them. Between their knees was a tiny table. Also between Oscar's knees were his ears. Little Janey's nose was running, the stream forking around her mouth to reconflux on her chin, flow upside down to her neck, and disappear behind the collar of a shirt depicting cartoon characters made of cheese. "Here," removing it from his pocket and setting it down, "is a delicious marshmallow. You can eat it now, if you wish. But if you can sit here for fifteen minutes *without* eating the marshmallow, you can have two delicious marshmallows..."

Little Janie never broke eye contact as she said, "Grown-ups lie," and stuffed the marshmallow in her mouth.

"I honestly thought this would take more time," Oscar said as he clicked the stopwatch. But he stood up, knees clicking, and opened the door, where the mother was chewing on something, making it difficult for her to talk.

She nevertheless immediately mumbled, "Where's my twenty bucks?"

"Dr. Jones will be right back with your emolument," offered Oscar, hoping that Erica Jones—not actually a doctor, but who is, nowadays?—wasn't planning on waiting fifteen marshmallow minutes: perhaps a bathroom break, perhaps (he now saw what Janie Sr. was chewing on; she had not even removed the filter) a cigarette break.

"I want my twenty bucks, jackass."

"I'll go get it," said Oscar with smooth assurance. He stepped back into the corridor, and saw Erica Jones coming along it.

"Okay, Pizzoli will see you. Hand over the clipboard and the marshmallow."

"She ate the marshmallow," Oscar said. "In [here he checked the stopwatch] one second."

Erica's pan darkened. "What? *You let her eat the marshmallow*? What am I supposed to do now? We're not budgeted for using a new marshmallow every time." She was shouting.

"But what do you do if the kid wants to eat—"

"We knock it out of its hands. I can't believe you let her eat the marshmallow!"

"Can't you just use the second marshmallow as the first?"

"You idiot! *There is no second marshmallow!*"

Just then the door opened. "I want my twenty dollars," said the mother.

"*They're still here?* You're supposed to get them out of the building—"

"I'm not going anywhere without my twenty dollars."

A hissing whisper: "—before they realize we're not budgeted to pay anyone twenty dollars."

The mother made a grab for Erica, and Oscar stepped away. He knew now which corridor Mr. Pizzoli was down. He backed up a few feet and gingerly set the stopwatch and clipboard down on the floor before he turned and—not *ran*, exactly, but hastened away. Erica's "Come back here" was strangled, possibly literally, in her throat. "Come bagggggghhhggher." Oscar did not. The buzzing and flickering light fixtures gave way to pitch blackness which gave way to a painful encounter with a door, which led to another corridor, which forked, one branch leading down to an impenetrable veil of shimmering argent concealing a void—*Better not go down there,* thought Oscar Cox, immediately forgetting what he'd seen—the other terminating in a door with a sign: *Anthony Pizzoli.* It was already half open.

· 4 · The rep · Gunogony continued · That tiny office · Rep · The conscious brain overruled · Always reject the first offer ·

**Antagony · Fraternal misunderstandings · Goat problems ·
Tip calculator · How are we going to get out of this one? ·**

Mr. Pizzoli hunched over a sweat-puddled desk and rubbed his
sweaty palms on his eyes like a man trying to knead himself
a different face. There was room in his office, in front of the
desk, for a metal gray folding chair, but there was no room for
a person to sit in it, if that person had legs. Oscar was sitting,
and had legs, and these legs were consequently side-saddle
with the knees braced against a cement wall. He longed for
the remembered comfort of that dollhouse furniture he'd been
sitting in minutes ago.

"I'm glad we have this opportunity to talk," Oscar said.
Genially.

"Wonderful, wonderful," said Mr. Pizzoli. "You're doing
great work."

"I'm doing no work," said Oscar. "I've been doing no work
for eighteen months, and I'm afraid I'm forgetting how to do
math."

"Don't do math!" Mr. Pizzoli said. "You don't want to cross
the Union by scabbing out some algebra problem in your spare
time."

"I don't do math."

"You'll regret it."

"I don't do math. But the thing is, I would like to do math. I
am in fact a mathematics grad student."

"You are. You are still a student."

"But I can't do math, you see. Because we're on strike." This
was true: All teaching assistants in mathematics (and geology)
had been on strike protesting some local bank employing a
janitorial agency that in turn used non-union trucking to...well,

16

the details were murky. But the T.A.s were on sympathy strike, and so they had remained.

"You're not on strike as a student, just as a T.A."

"But I can't really be a math student if I'm not allowed to do math."

Mr. Pizzoli kept kneading. He kept on sweating. His desk was completely covered with brown sandwich bags, but the sandwich bags were so greasy that the paper had become transparent, and you could easily see that underneath them were more sandwich bags. "Solidarity, you understand. Labor needs solidarity. Do you know how Poland got free elections? Solidarity. That's what you need the most."

"I understand that, but..."

"We've made great progress in the last eighteen months. We're getting close to a bill that requires children up to age ten to be restrained in child seats whenever they get in a car. After that we'll go for age thirteen, although some people think we can get up to sixteen."

"I'm not sure I get why that's progress," Oscar said. "Does the Union represent car seat manufacturers?"

For the first time, Mr. Pizzoli took his hands away from his pan. He looked right at Oscar Cox, and his beady little eyes were as red as rat's eyes. The pores all over his pan, for that matter, were the size of rat's nostrils. He had rat's nostrils all over his pan. "No, of course not. What would a bunch of T.A.s have to do with car seat manufacturers? No, no, we pass this legislation so people can't give each other rides. Not here, but Upstate; people drive cars Upstate. Where would be be if you could just give your friend and her eight-year old a lift to the doctor's?"

"We represent doctors?"

"No, we represent taxicab drivers. It should be illegal for

17

people to let friends ride in their cars! And now, at last, well, provided the friends are under the age of ten, it will be."

"It will be?'

"Unless they want to take the car seat out of one car, put it in another...we're working on legislation about that, too, so don't worry."

"Do cab drivers all have baby seats in their cabs?"

"No, they're exempt."

Oscar Cox tried to sit up straighter to regain command of this situation. "So am I on strike to protest people sharing their cars?" he asked.

"Not yet. No, this has nothing to do with you." Mr. Pizzoli leaned over, way over, sideways and pulled open a drawer. When he sat back up, he was holding a manila envelope. He weighed it in his hand, undid the string, and looked inside. Then he brought his hands down below the rim of the desk, where they could not be seen, and appeared to remove something from the envelope. He dropped the envelope, its red string still dangling, on the desk. A heavy clang as it hit, and a few sandwich bags billowed up and wafted to the sides of the desk where the walls prevented them from falling off. For the first time, Oscar realized that the only way for Mr. Pizzoli to get into his seat would be if he climbed over the desk, something he did not appear to be limber or spry enough to do. Perhaps someone lifted him up over it every morning and evening? "This," said Mr. Pizzoli, "has to do with the self-driving car."

"The self-driving what now?" asked Oscar, whose academic specialty was not futurology.

"What a nightmare it would be! I want you to imagine all the taxicabs, taxicabs driven by robots. Robots don't tell jokes! All the trucks, trucking along with no drivers. CB chatter dead.

18

Truckstop diners empty. What a godawful nightmare world. This is precisely what we have to stop."

Mr. Pizzoli paused here, his face too red and sweaty to continue, and Oscar felt that he ought to say something, so for lack of anything intelligent to add, he said, "There's certainly precedent. I believe many functions of the personal computer were held back for several years by the powerful concordance-printing lobby." He added, "None of this is crazy."

"Oh, we've had our eye on you, er," Pizzoli's eyes darted down to a scrap paperweighted by a chunk of donut, "Oscar. Your particular skills. At last you'll be able to do something useful with your life. You'll help out the working man, who is let me remind you the salt of the earth."

"Will it end the strike?"

"Sure, probably. But you have to do it anyway. You're the one who decided to join the Union."

Oscar had decided nothing of the sort. All T.A.s had to join the Union, and all math Ph.D. candidates T.A.ed. But he was not here to quibble. "I'd love to help," he said. "Perhaps your have a particularly tricky equation..."

"No scabbing!" roared Mr. Pizzoli as he upended the envelope. Out spilled (another great clang) a pistol and several bullets. You saw this coming, but of course Oscar did not, so he had a greater effort to maintain a poker face, as he realized he would not be regaining command of this situation. "We need you to kill Mordecai Johnson."

Unimpressed, insouciant: "Who's Mordecai Johnson?" If plussed is the opposite of nonplussed, Oscar was plussed, or at least he appeared to be. That was the poker in the face, and that was what Oscar could bring to the table.

"Some kid who's writing some nerd program that will let

cars drive themselves. So you don't need to have any moral qualms about killing him." Mr. Pizzoli pushed the pistol over with the eraser tip of a broken pencil. "Not that that should be a problem, as I understand it."

This was the moment when Oscar probably could have gotten out of things. He probably could have explained that they had the wrong guy and he had never killed a human being and probably never would, especially if someone invented a self-driving car and he never again had to wait interminably at a Jersey stop sign with his crazy fiance. But Oscar would not have been in this mess in the first place if he did not insist on hinting, or sometimes stating, that he had committed blood crimes for money. Once, some two years ago, a woman in a beer garden Oscar was climbing over the fence of had asked our hero if he had ever killed a man, and he had replied, "No, only women and children." Looking back, Oscar realized now that that was *the only time in his entire life* he had denied committing any act of murder. What was he going to do, stop pretending now?

"No problem at all," Oscar said, on pure autopilot, while his conscious brain kicked himself psychically in the seat of the pants and tried to think of a way to prevent this whole situation. Wasn't an autopilot just a primitive self-driving airplane? Shouldn't Oscar just kill this part of himself anyway?

The autopilot picked up the gun and studied it with a convincingly practiced eye. Obviously, the only thing Oscar knew about this pistol was this it was not a rifle. *What kind of gun was it?* A pistol. *What make, model, caliber, etc.?* You know those guns cowboys have, with a pearl handle, and a rotating cylinder? Not that kind.

It did have (Oscar noticed), rasped scratches over the metal, above the handle's pearllessness.

"You must think I'm an idiot," Oscar said, and set the gun on the desk. Despite the cavalier way Pizzoli had been tossing it about, Oscar figured it was not a good idea to drop a pistol in a tiny ricochet-room; he had no way, after all, of telling whether it was loaded, or if the safety, assuming it existed, was on. "This fellow has its serial number filed off. That's a rookie mistake. The first thing they do is look for the gun with no serial number. I'm not using this death trap."

"If you'd prefer to use your own..."

"I traded my vast collection of guns for heroin." Standing. "I'm sorry I wasn't able to help—"

But Mr. Pizzoli had drawn a second gun. I'm not saying he drew it and pointed it as Oscar, but it doesn't actually matter. He just drew it. It had been on his lap, and as it came above the desk rim, Oscar froze. He froze like a troll at cockcrow, staring stonefaced as his destiny crested the horizon. There it was. "Maybe this one will be better," Mr Pizzoli suggested in a voice that was less casual than it sounded. "It still has the serial number."

From his frozen half-crouch Oscar flopped back down again, "Excellent. Wonderful. Could not be improved."

"The details on Mordecai Johnson are in a folder in the envelope. He's coming to New York next weekend for a *tech-nology...conference.*" He said these words very carefully, as if unsure what they were doing in proximity to each other. He did not even try to pronounce the conference's name (Albiorix, according to the dossier, August 1st and 2nd). "It's at the Hell's Kitchen Sheraton" (he continued) "so there might be some security—but I assume that's where your expertise comes in."

I'm sorry but actually my boyfriend has a poetry recital that weekend is precisely what Oscar could not say at that moment.

21

Instead he said: "It doesn't sound so hard."

"We've made the right choice then. Johnson will be making a presentation at the *technology...conference*, and it's very important he dies before the presentation happens."

"I wouldn't have it any other way."

Pizzoli beamed. "You know, you'll be doing something really very special for organized labor."

"Splendid. I'm going to shoot him dead."

"You should be very proud. Of course, if you're caught, we'll have you killed in prison."

"I've never been taken alive," Oscar said, lamely. He felt ill. He had a little messenger bag with a water bottle inside, and a couple of wet wipes for his glasses, and André Lafon's *Jean Gilles, Schoolboy* (1912); now the envelope, still full of papers, a couple loose bullets, and the gun joined them. His shell of bravado must have shown a crack or two, because Mr. Pizzoli looked almost paternal, as he explained:

"It's for the good of labor. We figured you'd be the best choice, since you are fraternity brothers."

"Fraternity brothers?"

He glanced at his donut again. "You and Johnson. ΣΩΔ, at A—t College."

"I never technically pledged..."

He never technically pledged. But if he did not have sex with a goat, he had boasted dozens of times about having sex with dozens of goats. Goat orgies. Blind goat dates. Goats from underground. Goat-themed sex zeppelins. Goats' asses; asses' goats. All those filthy goat movies he'd invented and described the plots to in stomach-churning detail: *Deep Goat*; *Love Goat*; *The Goats and Mrs. Muir*. Resigned, Oscar Cox stood up.

Pizzoli did not, could not stand up. "Just in case you're

thinking of backing out, you should know," he said. His eyes for once did not look down; he had it all memorized. "You should know we have dirt on you. You were observed calculating a tip at a restaurant last Sunday. At Barb's. That's math."

"I assure you, at Barb's they put the tip calculations right on the receipt. There's no math involved."

"Well then." Mr. Pizzoli shuffled papers around on his desk, perhaps to look busy, but all the papers he moved were sandwich bags, so it didn't work. "That can be checked up on."

"One more thing," said Oscar, for he had many troubles and worries on his mind. "Is there...is there *another* way out? Of the building? A different way from how I came?"

Pizzoli kept shuffling papers, but he suggested a side branch in the pitch-black tunnel. This would lead to a staircase that hairpinned up to a metal sidewalk hatch. That would get him out under the scaffolding on the north side of the building; he just had to be careful of the construction workers there.

"Those construction workers. They're our Union, aren't they?" asked Oscar.

"It'd be hell to pay if they weren't."

"So, just curious. How come they're not on strike?"

Pizzoli crushed a sandwich bag in his fist. A trickle of grease leaked out between the fingers and slithered down his arm. "What are you, a moron? People *need* construction workers."

What do you do with a gun like this anyway? Do you paint the tip orange? Do you go down to the post office and sell it to whoever looks angriest? Do you slap a sticker of Walter Koenig on its side?

No, that would be too much. All of those are bad ideas.

What you do is you roll it in trash paper you yanked from the garbage and keep it with you at all times. You take it to dinner in Jersey. You take it back through the Lincoln Tunnel with its bomb sniffing dogs and (it was 2003, remember) its SWAT teams. You don't sleep with it under your pillow, because your fiance would probably say something. But you damn sure take it to brunch the next morning.

Barb's again, and it was always Barb's. They sat at the al fresco sidewalk section, and if anyone passing by had proved to be a violent madman, perhaps a Punic Nazi who burns babies for Moloch, but also just wants to burn babies, because he's a Nazi, then Oscar would once again have the opportunity to save the day, provided the Punic Nazi waited while he unwrapped the tissue paper and the grocery circular and the (this was new) cruddy old sweatshirt around all of it. Just an old sweatshirt in a messenger bag. No one was the wiser.

"Oh," said V.K. Kunti, and it was the *oh* of suddenly remembering. He asked Oscar: "Who's Malachi Johnson?"

The tea Oscar was drinking did not come out of his nose, but it went far enough along its skull route towards his nose that we could call it that. Oscar would have started coughing, except the tea was very hot, so he would have started screaming, except he could not inhale because he had to cough.

"No, not Malachi, something like that. Mordecai. There's some kind of dossier about him on our kitchen tab—*are you all right?*"

24

Oscar was not all right, but just then Andrew Schwartz—forty-five minutes late, as always—slid up next to them. This was so obviously aggravating to Oscar that the whole dumb-show writhing and gasping over a scalded nasopharynx could be passed off as an only slightly hyperbolic reaction. Schwartz and V.K. cool-bumped fists while Oscar recovered.

"Please try to have some dignity," said Schwartz.

I'm not saying an old hag had once cursed Schwartz such that if his lips ever touched each other his head would explode; perhaps one had and perhaps one had not. But Schwartz was certainly taking no chances, and for whatever reason his lips were always drawn over his teeth in a permanent sneer, or possibly grimace. Watching him attempt "Peter Piper picked etc." was...well, Schwartz would never try, but you could imagine what it would look like, and the imagining was unpleasant. He was, predictably, a failed actor, which was some relief, but he was also and subsequently a successful attorney, which was unendurable. Apparently attorneys never have to purse their lips. His entire legal career was composed of helping the heirs to the Robert Frost estate, to which Schwartz was only the most distant cousin, sue anyone who said "miles to go before I sleep."

"Technically," Schwartz was quick to point out, "that poem will not be in the public domain until 2019. It's a question of respecting the integrity of an artist's oeuvre."

Schwartz was a few years older than V.K., a few years less mature than V.K., but they had gone to the same Jersey high school and had a bond that being the only two out-ish gay kids in an early '90s high school will, apparently, give you. Surely there was no other way to explain why these two would tolerate each other.

25

"Have a seat," V.K. said to Schwartz.

"Are you trying to kill me? Sitting is the new smoking; no, thank you." And then, additionally, "Do you have any idea how much sugar is in that tea?" Schwartz sneered, or grimaced, at Oscar.

Now, Oscar knew exactly how much sugar was in the tea, because it is customary for the consumer to add his own sugar to hot tea, and, since it was green tea, the answer was no sugar. Furthermore, Schwartz frequently sat down, would in fact be sitting at this very table in a minute or two, and also occasionally smoked (at parties, or when nervous). But Oscar would not take the Schwartz bait and it was also still hard for him to talk. Undrained hot tea was still trapped in some pharyngeal oubliette, sloshing about. And Oscar had his eyes open for something that was not a Punic Nazi. He was looking for Susan Peters, who usually passed by on a Sunday, and usually stopped to say hello to Oscar and V.K., both of whom she only knew slightly, but slightly was enough to chat over the al fresco railing at Barb's.

Two things about Peters. 1. She was obsessed with Japanese comics about gay men, which was still unusual for a white girl in in 2003. Peters, approaching now in Hello Kitty overalls and a Rhoda Morgenstern headscarf, had scarcely been habituated to establishing future trends, but she'd be establishing this one. She'd have her time.

Also 2. she was a reporter for the *Post*. Which paper was one step above the *Weekly World News* or the *Police Gazette*, but it was still one step. Would ace reporter "Scoop" Peters be able to resist helping out a gay man in trouble? She would not.

Oscar stood up and stepped a few feet away, so he could intercept Peters before she reached the group. V.K. and Schwartz (now sitting down; of course now sitting) were talking, anyway, so from their point of view it shouldn't even look weird—just politeness, not to interrupt. Oscar, though, in a fit of cunning, touched Peters on the forearm upon interception and whispered to her with a sad look back at his companions, and implied heavily that the favor he was asking was a favor for all three of them. Would Peters be able to resist helping out *three gay men*? Fat chance! If she helped them, they might, in celebration, she doubtless imagined, all simultaneously kiss each other.

"I need a solid," whispered Oscar, as people used to do. The story he concocted, involving someone trying to frame some-one's brother (he left it vague) for shooting a neighborhood cat (?), did not have to make much sense, and indeed it did not, but it climaxed with the flourish/revelation of a 3X5 card onto which Oscar had copied an alphanumeric string off the pistol's handle. "Can your 'sources' trace this serial number?" asked Oscar.

"A car?" she asked.

"A gun," he said.

Oh, her "sources" could! This would be an easy task for "Scoop" Peters!

"Breathe not a word of this!" hissed Oscar; but also, "thank you."

Then they returned to the friends assembled, and Peters said hello and V.K. gave her a flier for his poetry reading next week; but Peters was buzzing. She was vibrating. She had a mission, and all these pleasantries were holding her back. She darted down the street as soon as she could.

"Who put the bee in her bonnet?" said Schwartz.

"So that kid," Oscar said to V.K., careful not to use names now that another witness was around, "he's a guy from my alma mater I'm supposed to go tutor. Don't tell the Union. Also I need to borrow your car."

"I can't believe," Schwartz was saying, gazing sadly at the two empty plates, "you bastards ordered without me."

• 6 • A brief history of mendacity • Plotz and counterplotz • Marvinless • The great secret • A reloading of the canon • That Oscar Cox! •

What kind of man was Oscar Cox? He was the kind of man who—but no, let us not pretend Oscar was a type. He shared characteristics with types, of course. He was a fraud and a liar. He was good at math. He lived in New York. But nothing about him added up to anything coherent. The series did not sum, which is a strange thing for a series not to do. We all like to think that we are unique, but being nothing is not exactly enviable, when you get right down to it. For example: Oscar was hardly really a man. He almost did not count as human.

There was always something a little dishonest about him, and yet young Oscar Cox never stole. He rarely cheated at games. He'd lie to get out of trouble, but no more than most kids. At a certain point he began to misrepresent himself. This was not always bad. When he was afraid he pretended to be brave. When he was unsure he pretended to be sure. Offered a cigarette, little Oscar said to the bad kids, as a demurral, "I've had to cut down to a pack a day, and today I'm already at my limit. It *is* almost noon, after all."

In the mornings, before school, he'd read in the newspaper the scores and highlights of the previous nights' sporting games, in case he had to pass himself off as someone who'd watched them. He read the last five pages of every mystery book in the library in case he ever had to pass himself off as a mystery-novel ("sure, I've read that one; quiz me if you don't believe") junkie. He memorized the number of steps in various stairways of various buildings (high school, library, church, grandma's house) in case he ever had to pretend to be autistic. He learned how to say "It cannot be revealed that I speak this tongue; tell no man that I have understood you; I must go now; say nothing" in fifty-odd languages. Perhaps someday he would hear two people speaking Estonian, grab one elbow, hiss his sentence, and run away.

"What did he say to you?" his friends would ask the Estonians.

"N–nothing. Nothing. But his accent was *perfect*."

Perhaps Oscar had always known what his great lie would be. But he was a lion, and must always pounce, even above the abyss. The summer before senior year, at math camp, Oscar's bravado managed to get him to third base with a curious trigonometrist. When Bugs Bunny thwarts the Martian, what does the Martian say? "There was supposed to be an Earth-shattering kaboom." But there was not.

"What's wrong?" she, the trigonometrist, asked.

There was supposed to be an Earth-shattering kaboom.

"I was just thinking of all the people I've seen die," said Oscar. "Sometimes their screaming faces haunt me."

What did the teachers say, when boys will be boys and brag before class? What did the teachers say about sex? "Those who talk the most do the least," they always bromided. And what did they mean by that really? The implication was: "See little Suzie in the ankle socks who sits there so quietly and primly? She must be a fuck machine," and this could not be right. Nothing anyone said made sense anyway, but nothing, nothing at all, had prepared him for the possibility of no Earth-shattering kaboom.

He braved out h.s. senior year, but college was traditionally a time to reinvent oneself. He thought he might try again little Oscar's cigarette trick, and act as though he was so weary from four long very horny teen-movie-style high school sex-romp years that he needed a sex sabbatical. But working this backstory organically into every introduction was wearying. It was easier to fall off the wagon. It was easier to walk into a room and tell everyone you'd just boned a lab assistant.

Which one?

"A gentleman never tells. We couldn't find a condom, so I managed to cram a test tube on..."

A gentleman never tells was the key verbiage, creating an endless orgy of anonymous and unverifiable couplings. If some Encyclopedia Brown pounced upon an inconsistency, Oscar could shrug it off. Of course he had to change small details to protect the...not-so-innocent (wink). Never doubt the power of the campy wink.

High school friends, e.g.g. Spanky Pair, Buddy Junco, Willie Verge, whose testimony might topple the house of porno-graphic French playing cards that Oscar had built up—those sex-romp years—had to be sequestered from all future ac-quaintances. Family, whose easygoing tolerance would be sorely taxed by the idea of a son snorting cocaine out of a hooker's butthole while whipping her with a shaved opossum ("we call that a Tuesday"), must be kept at arm's length. Enough A—t alumni made it down to New York that Oscar didn't have to start from zero in his post-Vera, newly out days. "You see that guy?" they'd say. "He'd pork a Berliner if it had a hole."

This was Oscar Cox's revenge on the world. But it was also (and some would say this was the nature of revenge) a pit he had dug that he himself had fallen into.

V.K. Kunti was, of course, Oscar's second attempt to escape from the pit. The first thing Oscar did, when they started dating, was jettison all the facts about sea life he'd kept swimming around his brain. And the next thing—for V.K. was pursuing a doctorate in English literature—was attempt to bone up on the centuries of canonical texts he had missed while restricting his reading to ("for ideas") de Sade, Sacher-Masoch, Krafft-Ebing, John Cleland, *Autobiography of a Flea* (1887), and George Bataille.

At first Oscar pursued his reading casually, but after the strike started, for want of anything else to do, he had really borne down. He never actually formed in his mind the words: "This will impress V.K.," but we all knew what he was up to. Because his learnery was based not on some syllabus but merely on his own hunches and vague impressions of canonicity, Oscar spent a lot of time mired in authors that were no longer widely read—John Greenleaf Whittier, Thomas Babington Macaulay, Lew Fucking Wallace—but such idiosyncrasy only gave a patina of verisimilitude to Oscar's pose as a well-read, well-rounded fellow.

Just a gentleman of leisure, struggling his way through David Jones's *In Parenthesis* (1937). As with The Case of St. Augustine, what a rakehell has settled down here! The heart of the prudent getteth knowledge; and the ear of the wise seeketh knowledge. What else was left for Oscar to seek?

So labour at your Alphabet,

31

For by that learning shall you get
To lands where Fairies may be met.

And going where this pathway goes,
You too, at last, may find, who knows?
The Garden of the Singing Rose...

...Andrew Lang wrote (1894) and young Oscar Cox memorized (1984).

"I heard Oscar Cox was in Algeria on a sex junket and managed to get the hostages freed."

"What? I'd heard that Oscar Cox was working for the Algerian separatists and he was the one who persuaded them to take hostages in the first place."

"Both of you are ape-nuts crazy, and there's no way that guy has even been to Algeria. Use your head! Although still." (Pauses, puts his hand upon his chin. Thoughtfully:) "There is something *about* that Oscar Cox..."

· 7 · The mountains of New England · What would Ritter von Niethammer do? · Same old A—t, same old world · Kick down the door if you must · A superflux of vulgarity · Plan A · As you know, the actual plan is to party ·

It's three long hours in a borrowed car if you don't get lost: up the coast of Connecticut to New Haven, and then I-91 all the way north. Oscar did end up a little lost, which was ridiculous because until the last fifteen minutes there was like *one turn*, total. But it happened, and Oscar snaked through strange mountains in the Bay State all morning long. The occasional decaying billboards bore ancient messages, never renewed, from politicians of long-forgotten election cycles (promising: "a chicken in every pot and a window to throw it out of") or Burma Shave. The valleys pooled with mist like ladlefuls of dry ice, and Oscar drove above them along hairpin roads, his trusty messenger bag by his side. A copy of Thomas Browne's *Pseudodoxia* (1646) was not all that was inside it. And the whole way Oscar wondered if he should, after all, kill Mordecai Johnson.

The obvious answer was *no*, but he was afraid of what would happen if he refused. Presumably the Union had people who would go after him in turn, and not all of those people could be fraudulent screw-ups. Also, the death of Mordecai Johnson would (Mr. Pizzoli had adamantly stressed) benefit immensely the cause of organized labor. How many coal miners died each year because the Unions were weak? Can we balance one life against theirs?

These were all bad arguments, but frankly, he knew the arguments *against* killing Mordecai Johnson were also bad. They were all based on the superstition that human life is important for some reason. Make no mistake: Oscar believed strongly in this superstition, but he could hardly prove it to be true in any formal sense.

He'd been to enough of V.K.'s departmental wine-and-cheeses in the last year to have heard, again, and again, that the enlightenment was a colossal blunder and individual life a bourgeois fiction. The last time he'd said the word *humanism* out loud, V.K.'s faculty advisor had assumed he'd meant it as in opposition to *feminism*. "I'm not a feminist, I'm a humanist, har har," e.g. This was not what Oscar meant, but by the time he's stammered out an approximated pronunciation of Pico della Mirandola, the offended professor had left in a huff. "I should have said *Erasmus*," Oscar thought, but it probably would have done no good. This, by the way, was when Oscar first began to suspect that his Western canon reading list was flawed.

But let's be frank. Let's be honest with ourselves for a moment. Oscar was not going to shoot someone in the head. Not for one minute, regardless of how much he wrestled with his bad angel in the Penuel ring, he was never, not in his wildest dreams, going to kill this guy. If Johnson came after him with a knife, sure, maybe he'd shoot him. He wasn't going to leave the gun at home, after all. If Johnson came after him with a knife everything would be much easier.

Still, best to come up with another plan.

It was summer, and why would Mordecai Johnson, or anyone, even be at A—t, instead of working a crummy summer job at the A&P? But Oscar had his dossier, and the dossier explained all: M. Johnson's habits, his weaknesses, the undergrad summer science program he was participating in. Since he'd be staying at ΣΩΔ house, the boy didn't even need to pay for a dorm.

Officially, A—t College had no fraternities, but officially the armed forces had no homosexuals, and that doesn't sound very likely in 2003. There were no fraternities on A—t campus, but there were plenty around its perimeter, and the school did not have a stance on whether students could join them in their free time. Students joined them, all right. For fifteen minute intervals, in the middles of the nights, these Greeks had been Oscar's court, fan club, and peanut gallery. But that was years ago. Now...now where did we put that nourishing mom?

Finally, finally a farmer (?) sporting what appeared to be false mustachios and a bad Maine accent appeared from behind a bush and pointed the correct way to A—t College.

"You look familiar," Oscar Cox said.

"Don't be an idiot, Cox," said the farmer, but with more of a Maine drawl, and hurried away.

And following the folksy (*turn left at the Guernsey*) directions, Oscar successfully slipped past the other nearby schools to the sleepy little campus of A—t. It all looked so similar, although he hadn't been back in five years. The nineteenth-century chapels and the twentieth-century monstrosities. The statue of Sabrina was still illuminated by floodlights around the barbed-wire-piled trenches. The statue of Noah Webster still lacked any such defenses. This was A—t.

Hanging from buildings were still abandoned, rainsoaked signs from the school year protesting the Iraq War. *No blood for bagels* one read, and Oscar had spent so much of his time in the tristate area that it took him a few seconds to figure out that *bagels* was metonymy for something other than *New Yorkers.* This, too, was A—t.

So little (we repeat) had changed. It was only 2003 but already the physical world had stopped changing: Cars looked like last year's cars, architecture looked like last year's architecture. Every year was copying off its neighbor's work. Already whatever fashion microtrends crept up, whatever the nowest haircut was—the afterrachel, the Hoboken asshole—it never trickled down from some mod elite to the regular joes, whose haircuts had frozen after the 'eighties and might now never change again. The sparse students looked the same as they had. Their tees and jeans looked the same. Their backpacks etc. It was as though it knew, the physical world knew that the countless millennia of its reign of terror were coming to an end.

The stately prewar Sigma house was off-campus, tucked

between Strong's Feather Boas Boutique and Imponet Construction Wholesale (corporate offices only); across the street was a Moishe Goldfarb's Cabinetry next to a Moishe Goldfarb's Intimate Apparel next to an Elks' Lodge; each building had a small parking lot in front of it—at least three bumpers by the cabinetarium bore identical bumper stickers: "My Boss Is a Jewish Carpenter"; and Oscar pulled up at the Sigma section.

He had never liked the custom of pausing a moment to "get into character" or "put his game face on." He firmly believed that he was always in character. So the moment the car stopped and the engine cut off, Oscar was out and striding with those purposeful strides to the overfull recycling bin around the frathouse side, to grab two reasonably uncrushed beer cans. Then purposeful strides again to the massive front door. He turned the knob gently and eased the door a quarter inch in, so the latch was sitting against the plate. Did he pause a moment at that point? We won't tell. But he did then take a step back and he did then kick the door in.

"Okay, fuckers," he screamed, "who's here to fuck?"

The door (as he knew it would) rebounded against the wall and came shooting back towards his foot, which was still (he'd learned so long ago) up to kick it back open. The Sigma house front door let to a marble hallway, but directly off that hallway was a large open doorway and a large room, the "study," that had held, and would probably always hold, 1. a television, 2. a ping pong table, and 3. the ineradicable and allied stenches of beer and vomit that crawled up one's nose and coated one's tongue and clung go one's hair. The thunder of that door rebounding off the marble wainscoting was tremendous, and the acoustics bounced that thunder right into the study. It took Oscar a few steps before he could see the results of his kick. And

36

there, in the great study, were six young men, all with wide-eyed looks of terror. Four of them were holding bottles of beer, and two of them had newly dropped bottles fizzing beer on their feet. They were all sitting in couches except one, who had leapt up and appeared to be looking for something to crouch under.

Oscar mimed chugging one of the empty cans of beer he held and then crushed it against his skull. "Is this all you motherfuckers are doing at four o'clock on a Monday?" he bellowed. "That had better be pornography on the television, or I'm going to boot up your urethras."

"B-boot up?" one asked.

"Boot. Vomit. It's a slang term that means vomit. I understand, it sounded like a computer term, or at least it would—*to a fucking computer nerd.* Is that all you are, a bunch of virgin nerds?"

"N-no." The lad actually stammered like this, like someone seeing Casper the friendly ghost for the first time. "Who," he added. "Who are you?"

A few fake sips from the second can, a can already open, as though he were a chain smoker lighting one cigarette off the last—only with beer. "Who am I? I'm Oscar fucking Cox, come to breathe some motherfucking life into you jackoffs!"

And that was the magic switch. They'd heard of him! He wasn't going to kill them and skin them and wear their skins (as one explained, unnecessarily, he had assumed for some reason). He was a friend, and more than a friend—he was a legend.

"You're a legend," another fratboy exposited, too late.

"They say that you banged every woman, and got so bored that you had to turn gay to get some sexual variety."

"They say that you were too much man for any woman,

37

and had to turn gay because it wasn't fair to the universe otherwise."

"It ill becomes one to boast," said Oscar modestly, "but let us say that there is a half truth in each of your observations."

"What's in your purse? More beer?"

"It is not a purse, it is a messenger bag, and it it filled with gay dildos. You shouldn't touch it unless you have built up an immunity to AIDS."

They all nodded to each other at this advice. It made sense.

"And what," the inquisitive little scamps continued, "are you doing here?"

Now this is where Oscar's plan came into play. All he had to do was somehow persuade Johnson not to come to the Albiorix Technology Conference in the first place. Then he could lurk menacingly outside the Sheraton all day and night, tell Pizzoli that the boy was a no-show, and go on with his life.

How to keep him away from New York? This might be as simple as getting his hands on Johnson's wallet, throwing all of his ID down a sewer. New York was in such paranoid lockdown that they would never let you take a bus into the Port Authority without a driver's license—which sounded like a weird way to go about things, now that Oscar thought about it, but there it was. Even if Johnson (in direct contravention of Mr. Pizzoli's desires) bummed a ride to New York in a friend's car, he would need ID to get into the conference, right? But that was dicey. That was only plan, like, E. Oscar would roll a blind-drunk Mordecai Johnson and huck his wallet in a sewer anyway, because better safe than sorry, but let's go with plan A. Plan A was to somehow elicit from Johnson his next-weekend plans. "What a coincidence, I, too live in the City! And I'll be passing this way next Friday..." Thereupon: Offer Johnson a ride, but on the day of the conference drive him out to a field in Pennsylvania (or somewhere), suggest a bathroom break, and then peel away, leaving a preferably walletless Johnson standing pants-down in a field with no way of reaching New York in time. Then: Stand outside the Sheraton etc.

All is planned out. All is clear. So let us return to the burning question:

What are you doing here, Oscar Cox?

"I'm here to party."

• 8 • **Antagony identified • Noms de guerre • Poisoning the well • Abortive sally • Car talk • Papers, please; no one has papers • Is this a murder hobo? • Not Oscar's most embarrassing secret • Plotinus would be a good example, or Porphyry • A new plan for the night •**

So. So so so. So which one of these twerps was Mordecai Johnson?

The dossier had a photo, of course, but it was a senior yearbook photo, high school, two years old and airbrushed. A suit and tie were involved. None of these zitty, rumple-shirted imps with the sleep crust dribbling from their eyes and forming a bridge or at least an archipelago with the food crust from the corners of the mouth resembled in the least that coiffed angel with the tasteful swirling blueblack backdrop behind him and soft-focus translucent larger floating head above him.

Oscar crushed the second beer can against his skull, frisbeed the disk at the TV to punish it (he explained) for showing a baseball game and not genitals, and demanded to know 1. where they were going to go drinking tonight and 2. who these

39

fraternity brothers were.

"Who? We're Sigma, the sum of all frats."

"I mean your names," said Oscar.

And thus he met Cody Ballentine, J.J. Thomas, Michael Wang, two guys whose names he could not remember, and, indeed, Mordecai J. Johnson, another little twerp with hair of a nondescript color, indistinguishable from the other little twerps except by the particular constellations of his acne. They did not call each other Cody, J.J., etc., though. Each had a ludicrous nickname, like Grundle or Choad. The one Jew was named Foreskin, but they quickly explained that his name was not in ironic counterpoint to, was in fact unrelated to, his heritage. "It's because of his face," said Fluffer (meaning Michael) and the statement, unfortunately for Foreskin, made a great deal of sense.

Rather than indulge in juvenile nickname humor, we will continue to call the brothers by the names their parents and the law have given them. Mordecai, who frankly had enough problems, we will forbear to call Scrote.

Oscar made himself at home. The frat house had been built at a time when even the drunkest college students had had fine taste in architecture, and the skeleton of the house was beautiful in a Silas Lapham kind of way. The staircases were marble, wide, and elegantly curved. The banisters were solid and the surviving balusters were turned in lovely amphora-like shapes. In every room, whatever crystal chandelier had once illuminated the place had been pulled down—in every room— by drunken Tarzans, but the wrought iron faux-ivy chains still swung in their memory. The ornate tin ceilings had proved inconvenient to vandalize, and still showed in their ancient glory. Everything else had been trashed. Doors ripped from doorways and then replaced with newer, cheaper, hollow balsa doors, which ended up smashed, their remnants still visible on the empty hinges, and replaced (in some cases) with beaded curtains. The moulding rotted off the walls, replaced with mold. Everything covered in a layer of poorly wiped-up vomit. It looked like Rome as Alaric left it. It was better than most, actually.

Oscar said he wanted "to mark [his] territory," and headed for the bathroom, with a secret side trip to the kitchen. The fridge, he saw, was filled with cold cuts, beer, a carton of OJ squatting guiltily next to a bottle of vodka, and old pizza slices sitting not on plates or even napkins but just on the grill-lined shelves, cheese oozing through the gaps; so he reached behind the appliance and pulled the plug. With any luck, Johnson would eat the tainted meat and get too sick to even think about coming to New York/a field in rural Pennsylvania.

This may sound cruel or irresponsible, but remember we're dealing with a kid's life. Surely the life omelet was worth a few salmonella eggs, and it's not as if these guys ever went a day without vomiting anyway. Oscar's conscience (more or less for once) was clear.

He came back with the vodka and he made everyone do shots out of Dixie cups.

"Should we do this?" asked the empty beer bottles, cans, and red cups strewn about the floor from the long day's day drinking.

"Beer and then liquor, get laid quicker," said Oscar.

"Liquor and then beer makes you queer," snickered Cody, who then got very red and awkward. Everyone took turns assuring Oscar that they were not homophobic in the least, and that they had nothing but respect and positive emotions for especially lesbians but also gay men.

The one grudging holdout was J.J., who said he certainly respected gay men but nevertheless admitted, disingenuously, that he wouldn't want his sister to marry one.

"Don't be a big dick, Choad," Cody hissed at J.J.

But Oscar waved away the offense. "I've choked down dicks bigger than that," he said. By constantly pouring drinks for his young charges, sometimes two at a time, Oscar was able to conceal—had had such practice at concealing—that the cup at his lips was never full, and never drunk. It was like a shell game, with the shells inverted. The ball was never where the mark expects.

"'And if it be not given us, then do we take it:—the best food, the purest sky, the strongest thoughts, the fairest women!' I quote Nietzsche. So anyway let's talk about what you guys are doing next weekend. Anyone going anywhere interesting?"

But the spirit of Oscar Cox had already descended upon the house. "Never think about tomorrow!" yelled J.J.

"Let's go out rip some bitches in half!" said Cody. "With our dongs," he elaborated.

"The fairest bitches," insisted Johnson.

Their first plan was to go to a strip club, which was very much not what Oscar wanted to do. So he said, "Let's save the strip clubs for another day. I could take you, in New York I could take you to strip clubs where the dancers are all cyborgs, their metal limbs clinging magnetically to the poles..."

"I'm not sure I could afford a cyborg strip club," Michael tentatively objected.

Oscar lay a paternal paw on his head. "Just photocopy some twenty dollar bills onto green paper before you go. In the dark, no one can see they're fake, and you can stuff them in G-strings all night."

"The photocopier won't copy money. It just makes a black box."

Oscar sighed. "Don't use a new photocopier. The ancient Xerox machine in the basement of the gym has been there since 1968, and it is doubtless still there. That will photocopy money, or pornography, or anything you want. But that will be another day, when you come to New York. Anyone coming to New York, incidentally, any time soon?"

J.J. pointed out—before anyone had a chance to answer Oscar's query—that the nearest strip clubs were far away and probably closed on the off season; and so consensus demanded a field trip, instead, to a local bar.

The good bars were also distant and not practicable to reach on foot. Several eager hands jingled out from pockets rings of keys, but everyone was already drunk enough that Oscar insisted they go in his car, which was actually his fiance's car, of course, and hardly suitable for six (one no-name lightweight had already passed out and was not coming along). But they piled in, and Oscar started it up.

"You should let me look at the engine," said Michael, who it turned out was some kind of car nut. "Hear that knocking? I can fix that knocking in fifteen minutes."

"Do not look at the engine."

"I can paint flames on the side of the car," he said. "You should let me paint flames on the side of the car."

"Do not paint flames on the side of the car. This car is stolen, and if I return it in precisely the same condition I got it in, no one will ever notice and it will be the perfect crime."

"Wow," said Mordecai Johnson.

They drove to a bar courtesy of Oscar's ineradicable muscle

memory, whereupon it was revealed, through the intermediary of an unamused bouncer, that the Sigma boys were all underage.

"We thought," J.J. said, his dewy eyes sparking red and off and red and off in the neon tavern sign, "that you'd know how to get us in."

"Obviously I thought you'd have fake IDs," Oscar said. "I didn't know your Hello Kitty wallets would hold nothing but Webelos membership cards." This was harsh, but he was working on something. The something was a plan. "I haven't been in this berg in five fucking years."

"Heh heh. Berg," giggled J.J., elbowing the one they called Foreskin.

Oscar ignored these juvenile monkeyshines. They all strolled around the sidewalks, as though looking for somewhere that would serve minors. "Now," our hero continued, "if we were in New York I'd get you into speakeasies where the hooch is so strong it makes you go blind temporarily and also super angry and the whole place is filled with blind people trying to punch each other and sometimes you're not even blind they just turn off the lights."

"Cool," Johnson cooed.

And so Oscar had to keep going, and every time he described a New York place he had to make it sound wilder and seedier. "I'd get you into a cock fight where the cocks have syringes full of adrenaline on their spurs, and they have to keep clawing and injecting each other until one of their hearts explodes."

"Ha ha ha! Boom!" said J.J.

"That's in New York, though. Out of curiosity, is anyone going to be in—"

"Hey, look," Cody said. He was pointing across the street at a panhandler. "Let's beat him up and take his drugs."

44

"We can piss on him," suggested Michael.

Oscar had his hands out in the whoa whoa pacifying motion, but, "You once punched a hobo I heard so hard," Johnson said to him, "his teeth got stuck in your fist, and when you pulled your hand away there were teeth in it, like he was biting your fist, and now he had no more teeth and you made a necklace out of them." Johnson seemed to be looking at the raised hands not for guidance, but for signs of scars.

"Well, now, I had a good reason to..."

"Never have reasons!" J.J. shouted. "No consequences!"

The frat brothers lined themselves up and carefully looked both ways, ready to cross the street and surround and assault and rob an apparently homeless man, aimless and alone.

"Remember, although we're still brothers, we can't call ourselves brothers when we're over there," Cody said. He turned to Oscar to explain. "We can't say we're brothers out loud in front of this guy because he's, you know."

"You never call yourselves brothers in front of black people?" Oscar asked, stalling for time.

"It almost never comes up," Cody admitted.

And the boys began to step, as one, off the curb. *Maybe I actually should shoot one or more of them*, Oscar thought. The gun was in his bag, and breaking up a hobo thrashing was a pretty good excuse for gunplay, both in the eyes of the law and in the eyes of Pico della Mirandola. But he would try something else first. He said:

"Before you go over there, my young friends, let me just say that I am disappointed in you."

"What? Nooo!"

"A gentleman does not spill the blood of the lower classes on the streets like a common ruffian. The police will come before you're even allowed to fuck the corpse. Instead, we must lure the indigent to a private club where he will be put in a cage and the attendees can cut him with a thousand razor cuts, while the orgiasts under the cage wallow in his flowing blood."

Starry-eyed, they asked: "Can you take us to one of these places?" What was wrong with these kids?

"Yes, provided you have fake ID."

"Awwww." For the first time, Oscar began to worry that it was possible he was a bad influence. He told the young brothers that he was going across the street to give the man a card for what purported to be a homeless shelter but was actually a snuff brothel. Then he crossed the street and surreptitiously handed over twenty-three dollars, which doesn't sound like much but was all he had.

Let us pause here, because these kids. What is wrong (to repeat) with these kids? Five years ago Oscar would have brought up a cock fight to *end* a conversation and get *thrown out* of a party (for the greater good, of course; for *reputation*: "Did you hear Oscar Cox was ejected from etc."). Five years ago he would have never compounded the words *snuff* and *brothel*. How could six people so innocent that they couldn't even successfully sneak into a bar, that they had nothing better to do on a Monday night than wander around town slowly sobering with a stranger—how could six infants be so jaded that the only way to stop them from hospitalizing a hobo was the promise that if they played their cards right they could see the man die?

For a panicky moment, Oscar worried that he was being played, that this whole fraternity, perhaps this whole campus, or state, was a cruel trick, and Mordecai Johnson would at any moment pull off a mask and it would be V.K. Kunti or Oscar's

46

mother or Oscar's eighth-grade gym teacher or (most likely) Mr. Pizzoli. "I knew it," would say the unmasked avenger. Everyone would know it except Oscar.

Oh, Oscar, you naive little infant yourself. The physical world had frozen solid, but any Neoplatonist will tell you that the physical word is but an illusion. Reality is elsewhere, and it was moving faster and faster.

Not that Oscar, in 2003, could have named a single Neoplatonist. That would come later. But it doesn't matter because these were not, after all, fake fratboys. Unlike some people, they were not frauds. With the exception of their names—not Grundle and Scrote, but their ostensibly real names—which have, we remind you, been changed, these were 100% real fratboys. Gospel truth. And they looked contrite.

"We hope you're not mad at us, Oscar," Johnson was saying.

"No, no, of course not. You have so much to learn. I will mold you into such rakes that I will step on your accidentally in the garden, striking myself in the face like a cartoon cat."

"Pax," Johnson said, and stuck out his hand.

"Pax," Oscar agreed, and then came the handshake, which quickly became too complicated for Oscar to follow.

Everyone looked puzzled. "Did they used to have a different $\Sigma\Omega\Delta$ grip in like 1970 or whatever?" someone asked.

Oscar shook his head and thought: "Seriously 1970 whazza?" but said: "No, what did you think? I'm not officially a Sigma brother."

"What!"

"I wasn't allowed to join for character issues. I was deemed too 'hard-core.'"

"Oh! You've got to let us initiate you!"

Oscar was walking back to the car, followed by his entourage of prospective initiators. "Don't be absurd," he said. He had already decided to abandon all plans, get in the car and drive away.

"You'd be our *brother*!"

"Shhh!" Cody warned, glancing back hoboward.

Oscar said, "If this is about fucking a goat, I assure you, I have already fucked the damn goat."

"You'll be reborn from the beer womb."

"You'll be reborn one of us!"

They passed a storm drain. "Quick," Oscar said, "Mordecai, give me your wallet."

"I didn't bring it because I knew I didn't have valid ID."

Other brothers still pleading. "Come on, man! You'll 'Σ! Ω! Δ! See the difference!'" Cody chanted.

"Wait, did you just say, 'Delta, see the difference'?" Oscar asked, pausing.

"Yeah, that's what the delta stands for."

"And earlier did you say sigma was the sum of all frats?"

"That's what the sigma stands for."

"Okay," Oscar said. "What's the omega for?"

"Join the resistance."

"Aha! Oh, out of curiosity: resisting what?"

"The...man?"

"Okay." Oscar let out a long, low whistle, the kind he'd read about in books. "Are you guys all physics majors?"

"Yes."

"Yes."

"J.J. is pre-law." But he wasn't actually. They just pretended he was because his name was John J. Thomas, and John J. sounded like John Jay. So J.J. said:

"Yes."

"I'm chem."

Everyone: "Loser!"

"I'm a computer science major," admitted Mordecai. "But I was afraid you'd make fun of me. *Boot up* and everything. I take a lot of physics courses."

Looking back on his college days, Oscar had perhaps been too focused on his own antics to notice that perhaps the reason he had spent so much time at Sigma O was that his classmates in the math classes had been pledges. And his classmates in the math classes were of course nerds. Could it be he'd only been impressing nerd frats all this time?

Look, if you're not a nerd, it's okay. The Greek letters are just bad puns, that's all. Omega is the symbol for ohms, the last word in resistance. At least now Oscar knew why they had no plans on a Monday night.

But you can't be too careful. As a test, Oscar said, to a random brother: "You! Who's your favorite doctor?"

Now, Oscar didn't know the "correct" answer. Maybe it was Dr. Dre, maybe that was too old a reference for college kids. But he did know what the wrong answer would look like.

"Tom Baker," said that guy whose name we have all forgotten. That was the wrong answer, the nerd answer.

And then Oscar had a new plan. He'd do their stupid initiation ceremony, during the course of which he would outdrink these nerds, whereupon a stupid drunk Mordecai Johnson would be like putty in his hands.

"All right, you virginos, let's go initiate."

· 9 · This is the initiation · Bound and blindfolded · Notice all these posters? Probably unimportant · Perhaps an irre-

**sponsible act · The beer womb · Eureka ignored · Rat Latin
· An opportunity to skip ahead · Iodine of a certain vintage
· A really very long catalog of ways to prevent yourself from
drowning, in an extremely specific situation ·**

"First we light the candles..."

"Fuck the candles! Everyone drink more beer! Mordecai,
where's your wallet, anyway? You said you were going to show
me your wallet. Let's get branded!"

Oscar Cox had acquired a football helmet someone'd left
behind a chair, and was wearing it—another old trick of his,
polytropic man of tricks. The faceguard made it impossible
for anyone to force alcohol down his throat, a real risk on the
frathouse circuit. It also made it more difficult for even keen
eyes to tell that Oscar was faking almost all his sips. His excuse
for wearing it, of course, was that he was already so blitzed that
he risked falling down and cracking his head open yet again.

"Got a plate in my skull," he explained. "Got it playing sports
in the war."

No one believed that, but you know how it works. They
believed it must have been something. Another good trick: Act
like the truth is too painful a memory to speak. "He said it was
sports in the war, but it must have been something so much
worse," is a sample sentence people might whisper about Oscar
later.

You know what was really very unclear? It was very unclear
whether the Interfraternity Conference would actually allow
these six underclassmen to initiate a post-graduate who didn't
even attend this school any more. It was very unclear whether
whatever went down tonight would be official. But most of the
participants were too drunk to care. Oscar was waiting to make

his move, although he was not yet certain what his move would be. Every move so far had been blocked. It was like playing chess with a bear. Perhaps you were the better player, but the bear just took your queen, I mean *took your queen*, and how are you going to get her back?

"We actually, um, Oscar, we don't actually do branding."

"ΣΩΔ is branded on my motherfucking heart!" said Oscar, and it was the mot juste. There was hardly a dry eye in the place. Cody vomited into a houseplant and Michael wet himself.

"I think to do it right we need to light candles."

"We know what you think, Foreskin. Stop being such a stereotype."

"Blindfold him and take him to the beer womb!"

"I'll get the human skull!"

"Are you guys even different people?" Oscar said. "Should I even try to remember which one of you says what, like there are different levels to your damnation?"

But then suddenly they had handcuffs on him. There was pretty much no way to blindfold Oscar with his helmet on, and he wasn't taking it off, so they threw a yellow-stained pillowcase over his head and spun him around and escorted him to a mysterious flight of stairs. Ahead he could hear Johnson falling down them.

"I'm okay, guys," Johnson called up from below. But his brothers had their own problems. They were rolling drunk and trying to lead a chained, blindfolded man who was, it turned out, the only thing holding them up. Oscar found himself supporting a half-dozen limp staggering idiots down steps he could not see, and doing it handcuffed. He started thinking that this one-story descent would be the hardest thing he would have to do all night, and of course with handcuffs on there could be no

51

knocking on wood.

At last they all found themselves treading on Mordecai Johnson, which meant they had reached the bottom of their flight. The pillowcase came off.

"This is the 'goat room,' the most secret place in the whole house," J.J. explained. "We're not even supposed to be here without a member from National overseeing..."

"And we're definitely not supposed to use the beer womb," added Michael, who had preserved his dignity by removing his wet pants.

"...but last time the National rep was here he got drunk and we stole his keys and excuse me I have to puke."

Oscar tried to tip an imaginary hat, which looked weird because of course he was wearing a real hat of sorts and also his hands were still behind his back. "Capital hijinks, my almost-brothers."

The room was, to be fair, somewhat neater and less vomit-encrusted than the rest of the house. It had a deep shag rug and cherrywood paneling. On the walls hung one poster of some 'forties pin-up actress with nipples drawn on her nightie in ballpoint and a crowd, a host of other posters for various televised special events: *Fox's Rock 'n' Roll Battle of the Sexes on Ice 4*, *The QVC 100-Product Showdown*, *It's Armistice Day Charlie Brown*. They went on and on. *The Monster Truck Rally Channel Presents Monster Trucks Rallying at a Monster Truck Rally. It's May Day* etc. Floor to ceiling, the posters. The house, it turned out, got free cable in exchange for hanging up advertisements, which they did in the most inaccessible room in the building as a pure dick move.

"I did say it's the most secret place in the whole house," J.J. said, wiping his mouth.

"I've only been down here once before!" Cody giggled.

The beer womb, turned out, was a gigantic deep freezer, the horizontal kind. "Just a point of information," Oscar said. "Wombs are supposed to be warm." But it was not plugged in. Also, holes had been bored in the lid...

"...so you don't suffocate," Michael, taking his turn on the carousel of exposition, said.

Oscar attempted to find a way to say, "I'm not getting in there," without sounding like he was pussing out, which was, of course, the one thing Oscar Cox would never do. But, really, what was the advantage of getting into the beer womb? How would this help his plans? "Drink more beer," Oscar instructed, but they were not drinking their beer. They were pouring their beers into the beer womb. But the freezer must have held 150 or 200 gallons, and they simply did not have that much beer. Where did they even get the beer they had without a fake ID?

"National provides each chapter with a beer ration, regard-less of age," Michael said in his underpants. Technically it was not his turn.

So after filling the beer womb an inch deep with beer they surrendered to necessity; and thus began the unfortunate spectacle of the boys of marching up and down the stairs with buckets of water. They were not in marching condition. They had no Oscar to help them up and down. The water went everywhere. The buckets went everywhere. Flailing soggy limbs cartwheeled, again and again, down the stairs. But still these merciless sorcerer's apprentices came, and the beer womb began to fill, and certainly it was not warm, and, "Don't fill it past the red line or he'll drown," someone said.

"I'm not getting in there," Oscar said, flat out, but they were no longer listening, and there were six, however drunk, of them, and they had arms. They were so serious, their sagging bodies weighed down by the gravitas of this ancient ritual in its ancient Frigidaire. There was also a human skull involved. Like a virgin borne to the volcano, if the volcano was only four feet away and very wet, Oscar went.

And then Oscar Cox was under water.

"Oh no! It's over the red line!" Various bailings. "Why are my feet wet?"

Oscar was about to point out, perhaps rudely, something about physics, but a bucket hit him in the head—bounced off the helmet, he was fine, but if forced him down under the water.

Dimly he could hear someone intoning bad Latin, not pig Latin or dog Latin but like rat Latin. "In lemonade potty." It may have been a blasphemous parody and it may have been the game-of-telephone of several generations of non-Latin speakers trying to remember a series of syllables. One hundred and fifty years after the Napoleonic Wars, the children of the Danish island of Anholt still sang the nonsense rhyme their great-great-great-grandparents learned from occupying British soldiers:

> Jeck og Jill
> Vent op de hill
> Og Jell kom tombling efter.

And perhaps everything is just the perverted memory of an order that once made sense. Perhaps Oscar would have plenty of time to think about such things, or similar things, as the lid came down with a snap.

"Drink to the womb of beer!"

"To the North and to the South!"

"Sing praises to ΣΩΔ!"

All together: "ΣΩΔ o' you! ΣΩΔ o' me!"

"Glub," said Oscar in his womb, his head still under water.

Because the womb of beer had been carefully planned out. Nobody wanted another fraternity death so every hazing ritual was test-marketed and safety-checked like a Disneyland ride. When the womb was filled to the red line, the pledge-fetus had enough room to extend his face above the surface of the beer, breathe the pure serene air of the most secret part of the ΣΩΔ house. Stay, in other words, alive, as his toes wrinkled and puckered. This was how you did things.

Unfortunately for everyone, Oscar was wearing a football helmet. It had seemed like a good idea at the time, and it had probably left him in a soberer state that he would otherwise have been. On the other hand, the faceguard clacked against the lid and in vain the holes in his pan sought to breach the surface of the liquid.

What follows will be a long and fairly detailed account of Oscar's attempts not to drown. It will not be an overly technical account, as, if there exists trying-not-to-drown jargon, which there might not, it does not get bandied about in this book. There will be, as per Union rules, almost no math. But there will be detail, and if, by chance, you have no interest in what one might try to do while stuck in a coffin, essentially, filled with water, you can take as a summary: "Oscar tries really hard not to drown, and it is not going well" and skip to the final two paragraphs of the chapter to learn if he survives. This book is a thriller, after all, and a thriller cannot get bogged down in long descriptions. *The weather was: fine. His clothes were: wet. Oscar was...*

...drowning. Through the dulling walls of water and the

55

padded walls of helmet he could hear these physics lads, these Baryonic heroes, these Niels Boors, chanting "chug chug chug," and at first he thought that they were suggesting he drink enough of the water (with trace amounts of beer) so as to lower its level, but as he tried to figure out whether his expanding water gut would displace enough mass to keep the water level steady, he realized they were chanting not to him but too each other. Since they'd poured all or almost all their beer stores into the womb, Oscar knew, having taken informal stock of their alcohol options earlier, that they must be chugging 1. tequila, 2. rubbing alcohol, 3. iodine, or 4. gin, none of which sounded like really super good ideas.

In desperation Oscar tried the drinking trick, but it quickly became clear that he would only be able to get down a half pint or so before he died. So then—and let us reiterate that he could not breathe—panickily, Oscar started sloshing his body to one end of the freezer and then pushing hard with his legs to move quickly towards the other end. The freezer was scarcely five feet in length, so he did not have a lot of room, doubled up as he was, to slide back and forth, but he compressed his body as best he could, and then pushed off as best he could. The water inside the womb moved as his body moved, and for a dim moment the amplitude of the wave was positive enough by his knees and negative enough by his head that he could draw, at last, a breath. He repeated the motion a few more times until he no longer felt like he was in danger of passing out. Then he husbanded his breath and when the amplitudes were right he tried calling out that he was drowning.

The sounds he was hearing, all around him, were hardly the kind to brace up his courage. Someone was snoring loudly, probably more than one person. Someone was yelling: "Look at me, guys!" and then someone, perhaps the same person, was vomiting. It sounded like several people were laughing their incoherent way up the staircase. No one, of course, was listening to a drowning man.

And the thing about the underwater calisthenics Oscar had to do every time he wanted to breathe—they were extremely tiring. The more he did them, the heavier his breathing became. So he had to do them faster, and then his breathing became heavier. He could see that this gyre was going to perne, excuse me, *turn* or (better) *spiral* out of his control. There would be no escape from this dialectic, no matter how much Oscar flexed his Hegel muscles. You see what I'm getting at, here: Oscar was going to die.

So a new plan: Oscar held his breath, braced his back against the floor of the freezer, and brought his legs up, with some twisting difficulty, into the fetal position but with feet planted against the lid. He pushed, but indeed it was locked. If ever he was going to be able to exert a herculean effort and shatter the freezer asunder, it was not going to be while out of breath and with head underwater.

So a new plan: Oscar tried contorting his body. The helmet prevented his lips from reaching air if he floated on his back, but by arching that back and turning his head upside down so his neck pressed flush against the lid, his Adam's apple poking into one of the air holes for extra wiggle room, he found that with his mouth opened wide, his chin and the chinstrap likewise flush on the lid, his jaw and in fact part of his gaping mouth was in the air. Of course, water still filled his mouth, but by using his tongue he could eject the water long enough to take a deep breath. The timing was dicey, though, and after only a minute or two he inhaled some water, and began to choke. To prevent himself from drowning while he coughed, Oscar returned to the calisthenics. When he recovered he arched his back again, which, as you might imagine, was extremely uncomfortable. The underside of the helmet's faceguard levered itself against the lid, making it harder to stay in this position than it would have been. And then he inhaled some water again.

Clearly he would not be able to keep this rotation going until the slumbering jackanapeses sobered up. But Oscar had long ago learned to assault a problem in different ways, from different angles. So a new plan: After a successful deep breath he sank his body to the bottom of the freezer (no mean feat itself with lungs full of air) and felt around behind him with handcuffed hands. After three refills and four descents he fumbled across the very thing: a drain for defrosting. It took him two more refills to pull out the plug (he had assumed, erroneously, that it would screw off). The look of triumph when it popped free!

But the water did not drain. Not all but many freezers, including this one, have a second plug on the outside (where you're supposed to thread a hose) which must also be removed. Oscar did not know that at the time, but it was not hard to guess. He tried snaking his fingers down the drain hole, to push the plug out from inside, but it was too far to even touch, let alone push. He tried cupping his palm and pushing it against the drain, forcing water through in an attempt to pop the external plug, but this, as you can imagine, was tiring yet accomplished nothing. He tried to persuade himself that the slither of water that went down the few inches of drain hole might have lowered the level enough to make breathing easier.

It did not. But it gave him an idea. He kicked off his shoes. First one sock and then the other he worked off with his toes.

With his face submerged he forced a sock, by toe strength, up through one lid hole. Water from the sodden sock, as he pushed it with his toe, oozed out onto the freezer lid. Some dripped back down through a neighboring hole, but some must have trickled off the side. He soaked the sock, while breathing upside down, and then forced the sock up again. Perhaps if he kept this up he would be able to lower the water to a comfortable level where he could just float on his back and breath easily and only worry about freezing to death in this cold tapwater. Perhaps just four or five thousand more sock wrings...

Just then the freezer jerked. Someone was rocking it back and forth, which could not have been easy—with water and Oscar in it, the whole contraption could have massed half a ton. But the rocking was only enough to move it slightly (if Oscar's estimation was correct) away from a wall. Then an audible pop as the outside plug was drawn. The water drained with a sigh.

Ragged, wet, and out of breath, Oscar lay at the bottom of that empty, cold, uncomfortable freezer. "Hey!" he called. "Let me out!" But no one let him out. There was snoring all around him. After a while he stopped yelling and allowed himself to slip into a shivery half-sleep.

· 10 · Aubade · Yet another complication · Revenge · Driving naked · Get off my lawn · Life among the plants ·

At last the dawn came, or *possibly* the dawn came—in a windowless basement room a lark's as good as a nightingale. But whether it was dawn or not, it was the time when Oscar's kicks and cries roused the sterling lads of $\Sigma\Omega\Delta$. The locked lid opened. The candles were burned out. It was more or less morning.

59

"Man, you are lucky you're not dead," J.J. Thomas said. More or less dawn, but the only envious streaks were on J.J.'s underwear which the brother was wearing on his head. He was wearing nothing else. "We totally should not have left you in there all night."

The shag carpeting all around the beer womb was a swamp, and everyone who stepped in it complained, "My socks!" except Oscar, who was, after all, soaking wet, sockless, and, as the difficult clamber out of the freezer emphasized, still handcuffed.

"How did you get the water out anyway?" Cody Ballentine wanted to know. "How'd you open the plug?"

Oscar looked around to see if anyone was going to own up. He could see, now, that the external drain had been braced against a wall (the absolutely stupidest place for it to be), so he'd had no chance on his own; but somebody had, somehow, inched the heavy freezer over; somebody had popped the drain.

"I fucked it," said Oscar, predictably. "Now get the cuffs off me." But whispered consultation indicated that Michael had the key. Which would not have been so bad, except he and Mordecai Johnson had left, an hour or more ago, to spend a week at Michael's parents' house in Dutchess County, New York.

"Johnson went where?" demanded Oscar.

The lads were busy murmuring their gratitude that their chums had slipped away silently, leaving the rest to their beauty slumber, but they paused to answer Oscar's more pressing question, even though technically they already had.

"He went with Fluffer [Michael Wang]. They're gonna hang out for a week and then go to the tech conference."

"That's ridiculous! How can he just leave for a week? Doesn't he have responsibilities? What about his summer program?"

"That ended three days ago. It's almost August now." And Oscar realized he should have read the dossier more carefully. "Oh man, Oscar. We can't drink like that when we're *studying*!"

Now, this was all happening, please recall, in the most secret part of the frat house, so Oscar couldn't even leave until they'd blindfolded him again. This time they took the helmet off. J.J. wanted to use his undies as a blindfold, but Oscar kicked so violently that they finally dredged up the same filthy pillowcase they had last night. Up the stairs, and when Oscar was unmasked he was dripping water on the study floor. A hacksaw did cut the handcuff chain, which was something, although Oscar now had two irremovable bracelets. His wallet had pretty much disintegrated, but everything in it that really mattered was laminated, and survived—he'd already given away his cash, but he pretended that a wad of bills had come to pieces in the long soaking hours of night and floated away, and thus managed to bum a few bucks for tolls and gas. Still in his wet clothes he drank about a quart of warm orange juice for breakfast and then bid everyone good-bye. It was very subdued. Oscar was very subdued. He was uncharacteristically silent

"He must have one hell of a hangover," one brother assured another.

"He sure earned it," the other brother reassured back.

Oscar considered saying, "You might want to plug your refrigerator in," and then decided that revenge was a dish best etc. Room temperature, maybe. And he said nothing. That was the sort of man Oscar was. The brothers gave him money and orange juice and he said nothing.

He shuffled outside into the merciless brightness. A crow was sitting on V.K.'s car and as Oscar shooed it away it quacked at him. It flew off and quacked, which we all know is not the sound a crow is supposed to make, but there it was. Quack.

Oscar stripped down in the lee of the car and threw his clothes in the backseat on top of his messenger bag to dry. He let the summer sun, streaming through the windshield, weigh upon his body like a comforting incubus. If he was driving home from a wild night, buck naked except for the handcuff remnants — well, was he not Oscar Cox?

And what had he learned from his little adventure, and the almost dying and all? He'd learned that already some vast cloud of unknowing had descended between him and the next generation. He's always been aware this would happen, that first his slang (*radical! tubular!*) would sounds as dated as a *Lord of the Flies* character's, and then his ironic use of intentionally dated slang (*ginchy! quite the berries!*) would stop sounding intentional or ironic. While he'd been doing and then not doing math, a secret Battle of the Somme had silently blown a yawning chasm between his age and theirs. Something had happened, some terrible falling away, and now history had crossed a watershed. The rivers ran backwards. Oscar shielded his eyes but he could not see the other side. He was in his late twenties. Oscar had grown old.

For some small time he could cash in on his virtues: 1. he lived in New York City and 2. he was good at lying. But eventually even his lies would cease being attractive.

This was the true fiction of Dorian Gray—not the immortal-painting part, which may or may not be plausible, or the gay curios, but this: Dorian died in 1890; by the end he must have been complaining like an old fart about the Impressionists and whatever happened to *normal* paintings with *sharp edges*? and *real* women wore *bustles*, didn't they? and if he had survived to see the twentieth century he would have been that much worse. Dorian was living on borrowed time, but back then it was less clear. Back then it seemed the physical world changed as well, and if you could just halt it you halted everything. *If we glue the leaves back on the trees, winter will never come.*

The rolling hills and the summer greenery was all around, and Oscar remembered what Vera Rodriguez used to say when presented with such a spectacle, the forested glory of the Bay State's natural splendor. "This place is not for us," she would say. Because everywhere the water was so teeming with animal life, with schools of fish zipping all around the krill and the coral, while strange visitors, gulls or otters, swept in and out, returning with their plunder to a hostile land, not their own. Here on the land, in the cruel sunlight, everywhere there is a plant, and animals merely flit and skulk in the plants' shadows; while in the sea, where animals belong, the power dynamic, or even just the mass ratio, is reversed. A car drove past with a hand-made sign adhering to, and mostly blocking, the rear window: *No Maslems! Towl head's go home!* So little animalia in this, the enemy's territory, and one of them had stopped and made a sign. And that sign, too, was 2003.

Oh, Oscar had a long time to think down I-91. And sometimes he thought he should try to dig up Mordecai's location—the Wang house—in Westchester and warn him, and sometimes he thought he should just keep driving, driving on and on through plantland after plantland. Sometimes he wondered about killing people, which along with being able to change a flat tire and build a house was a skill that men of previous generations (as depicted on television) took for granted, but which Oscar lacked. Could it be that assassins, like carpenters or, perhaps more saliently, like cowboys, understood something about the

63

human condition that the unblooded never would? But then Oscar had the thought: What if someday he shot someone point blank, and the mark just batted the bullets away and laughed, and then, right before he tore Oscar in two, he said, "Oscar Cox, you poor fool, you never understood anything"?

What then? Oscar looked around for any farmers in mustaches, but there was nothing. He made his sole turn, which was hard to miss as the only other option was to drive into the sea, and then he sped down the coast until the great tangle of ramps and overpasses crowded out all other scenery, and then on into the city proper. If Oscar said, "This place is not for us," he didn't mean New York City, and he didn't mean the Triborough Bridge, and he didn't mean Queens, the Ugliest Borough. But he didn't not mean them either.

Stopped in traffic in the early afternoon along Astoria Boulevard, naked driving seemed like less of a good idea. But Oscar rolled down the windows and acted like it was all part of his plan. His lifelong plan. In a roundabout way it was.

2

Book II: The Moderate Orcana

This is the World that opens and shuts like the Eye of the Wax Doll—
—Emily Dickinson, letter to her sister

· 11 · The secret to making a great cup of pu-erh tea is to go light on the rinse, and then steep the leaves for like five times longer than anyone would suggest; the tea will become pitch black and as thick as blood, and you may only get one cup from the leaves but it will kick like a mule ·

Oscar was home and showered and changed and prepared by the time V.K. came back from the library. *Welcome home,* each could say. They sat out on the balcony, which was actually just the roof of the building next door, one story lower and accessible from their kitchen window, drinking hot pu-erh tea and looking out at the fumes coming off the East River. Oscar used a Booth Tarkington novel as a coaster.

V.K. and Oscar shared a pretty nice one-bedroom walkup, fourth floor of four, in one of the crummier parts of Astoria, Queens. Split the rent, and it was affordable. One tenant could do work on the couch, while another did work on the futon, which was also their bed, and even the late nights' reading didn't bother anyone. It was a full twenty-minute walk to the subway, but there was that beautiful view over the river. The paint was full of lead and the stairwell was full of silverfish and the shower was full of mildew, but the balcony was only full of all the filth and miasmas of the Greatest City in the World.

"How'd the teaching gig go?" V.K. asked, and did Oscar improvise an answer? He did not, because he knew well this question was coming. No improv needed. Oscar was guarded; he was *semper* prepared.

"It was terrible," he said, and that's the thing. You start with the truth.

"How is it you were allowed to do...you know...'son of Mathonwy'?" V.K. had read the *Mabinogion* during an abortive study of the works of William Morris, so Oscar, too, had read the *Mabinogion*. The one-syllable name of Mathonwy's son, used to avoid mentioning the tabooed word, should not be hard to guess.

Oscar said, "Let's say hypothetically you're a union boss and you have a hypothetical kid who's struggling in the son of Mathonwy. Perhaps you'd strongly suggest it's in someone's best interest etc."

"Ah. But the hypothetical kid was innumerate?"

"No, no. He was smart, he knew his stuff. He was just a drunk."

"You used to be a wild, hatless little savage yourself, as I understand it."

"I don't want to sound like an old man. I hate it when people call me old man..."

"Even Victorian hunters at the club?"

"Even Victorian hunters at the club," Oscar agreed. "But nevertheless...kids these days!"

"'With their video games and their rap music.'"

"I don't understand them and they don't understand me. Among the things they also don't understand is everything."

"Do you want another cup of tea?" V.K. stood up.

"No, I'm...I'm still brewing." Oscar struggled to express his frustration with the night-before in ways that would conceal the fact that he had almost died and also the fact that he had more or less promised to help some teenagers kill a hobo and also the gun and also everything about what happened. He also wanted to avoid sounding like his grumpy old grandfather, or grumpy old Dorian Gray, which he completely failed to do. He wanted to say (he was trying, through the open window) that at a certain point, if you cut yourself off so hermetically from human experience, you were no longer human yourself, or were only human in the physical, disgusting ways. That if you presented these boys with a classic text—*Othello*, say—they would scratch their heads and say, "I guess Othello is jealous... because Cassio and Desdemona wouldn't let him watch? Jeez, just buy a camera, Othello."

V.K. had reappeared with a steaming cup. "You talked about *Othello* with the hypothetical?"

"No, but...hypothetically yes."

"I suspect the only difference between these kids and us is that there was a point in our lives when we had to struggle to see pornography, and not for one moment of these kids' lives has that been true."

67

"I'm sure my grandfather would have said the same thing about us. 'In my day we had to order circus magazines from Sweden just to see a girl's legs in a leotard.'"

How did V.K. end up here, the double beard on the rooftop balcony? Their first date had been a deadly boring foreign film, and as they left, Oscar had sneered sarcastically, "Chills ran up my spine."

"All the way to your face?" V.K. had asked.

Face, why face?

Because that's where the spine ends. "Because," said V.K., who was not yet at the height of his powers, "the face is the spinal frontier."

Was their future cohabitation and engagement foreordained from that moment? What if (Oscar had often wondered) he had said, instead, that chills had run down his spine? Where would we be now?

"And the new bracelets?" V.K. was asking, tipping his mug wristward.

"A gift from the Union. If the kid passes, they come off."

"'Hard core.' Are you sure you didn't spend the night in a police cruiser? Are you a fugitive from the law?"

"I assure you, I have an alibi. The whole A—t campus can attest to my innocence. It's summer, so that's only like forty people, though."

"I believe forty alibis is called an Ali Baba," said V.K., who could not resist smiling at his own joke. He hid his pan behind steam, but his eyes, visible as through the mist, were smiling. His eyes were cracking up. "When," he continued, "'s the big test?"

The big test. Oscar could hear the falseness in this excuse. The 'big test' you had to pass was a sitcom contrivance. It was the end of July, what big test could a college kid possibly be taking? He wondered if V.K. could hear it, too, as he said it, the convenience and the falsity and the...

But all he said was: "Friday. So if you're asking if I'll have them at the recital, the answer is hopefully not but maybe."

"I'm sure they're quite fashionable."

"You nervous?" asked Oscar, who had been in one nonstop nail-biter tear since he learned about the assassination.

"Well, I've already memorized the piece, obviously."

They clinked steaming mugs of pu-erh and Oscar worried and worried into the night.

• 12 • **Early frost** • **The boards did shrink** • **Nomenclature** • **TANSTAAFL** • **A lead, most definitely** • **Mousetraps, etc.** • **Nevertheless, it moves** • **Most of an unpleasant meal elided** • **Schwartz to the rescue** • **Preparing for the morrow** •

On Wednesday, Schwartz wanted to celebrate a "big [law-case] win," so he came over to take V.K., and by extension Oscar, out to dinner. Apparently some graduation speaker at some podunk college had said, "And that has made all the difference," and Schwartz had been there to pounce.

"The hilarious part," Schwartz said first thing as he walked into the apartment, "is that the guy settled right away, but that whole poem is public domain. If it had gone to trial, he would have learned right off he didn't owe a cent."

Second thing Schwartz said, to Oscar, was, "You know, the whole health benefits from drinking water is just a load of hokum. It does nothing for you."

Oscar, yes, had been standing in the kitchen with a glass of

69

water in his hand. "But I was thirs—"

And now Schwartz was talking again about his legal victory. He wasn't even looking at anyone as he talked, he was just picking things up and inspecting them—the Elizabeth and Darcy salt and pepper shakers, the vintage promotional photo of a tuxedoed Cary Grant in a pewter keepsake frame (a Christmas present Oscar'd given V.K. a year and half ago), the pressed cakes of tea that were not hashish but which, Schwartz's raised eyebrow implied, resembled hashish—without stopping once.

Oscar was ready to go, but V.K. excused himself to go to the bathroom. The bathroom was down the hall, so everyone was spared the hovering, wavering door dance.

That left Oscar with this nonstop pill. "Why," asked Schwartz, "does V.K. always have to hit the can before we go out to eat?" he asked. "It's like a pathology."

"It's efficient," Oscar said. "He hates to wa—"

"It's a pathology is what it is."

Fearing that anything he said would get cut off in the middle, Oscar silently slid a program out from underneath a fridge magnet and handed it over. Schwartz glanced down at the folded paper with a puzzled expression. He always appeared confused when he wasn't talking—worse if someone else got a chance to speak—but maybe (Oscar hoped! let him hope!) Schwartz was just illiterate. It would explain so much!

"You going to his recital?" Oscar asked, taking advantage of Schwartz's puzzlement to complete a sentence.

"Yeah, yeah," he said. "What's this, here: 'V.K. Kunti'? V.K.? Look, it's one thing to go by his initials in daily life, but don't you think it's a little misogynistic for him to use his initials in his writing?"

"Maybe you should ask hi—"

"E. Nesbit, J.K. Rowling. Fine women writers have always used initials as a shield against the patriarchy. The idea of V.K. co-opting their defense is really offensive."

Oscar could not think of something he wanted to discuss less, but then he remembered The Case of the Road Not Taken and realized that, yes, he could, so he said, "But look at V.S. Naipaul or R.K. Narayan. It seems like a common Indian thing."

"Native American."

"What?"

Schwartz rolled his eyes. "Indigenous peoples prefer *Native American*. Jesus, what's wrong with you?"

Before Oscar could offer a rebuttal, V.K. came back from the bathroom.

"Why do you always stop in the can before we go out to eat?" Schwartz demanded.

"I don't really enjoy washing my hands," said V.K.

But Schwartz was off on something else. "Good Lord," he cried, pointing to some loose tea leaves on the counter. "Are those rat droppings?"

They were not. So the three walked to Barb's, because they always went to Barb's. Peters was there with her old college roommate, Angie Toole, and Oscar could just make out what they were saying as he pushed the door open.

Angie: "It's just, like, what if I want to watch a World War II submarine movie?"

Peters: "I really liked her art when she did crosshatching. Oh! Oscar! I was hoping you'd show up here." Peters got up and took Oscar by the arm. There was only a moment of hurried logistics—V.K. and Schwartz would go look for a three-seater—before Peters drew Oscar away.

"Look," Peters said. "I've been digging into your brother's

pistol." (Who cared how she remembered the vagaries of that cover story?) "It's weird. I mean, it's registered, I've got an address, but there's something strange about the whole thing."

Just then a man with a clipboard strolled over, as though he'd been waiting. "Excuse me," he said. "I'm doing a test of basic astronomical literacy among Americans aged eighteen to thirty-four. Very quickly," addressing Peters, "would you say the sun rises in the west?"

"What? No," Peters said. "The sun rises in the east."

"I can quote you on that?"

"Yes, of course."

"Thank you." And he was gone.

Peters watched as the cafe door dinged shut. "See, weird things like that have kept happening to me the last two days. Anyway, I have the address, it's in Manhattan, 451 W 55th Street, but it seems to just be a fake address for a shell company called Eradication Age. They're just a name, they don't do anything, they don't make anything, but they're owned by a company called 2401."

"That's 7^4," Oscar said, without thinking, and then looked nervously over his shoulder.

"Well, that's something, at least. Because 2401 is also a fake company. All they do is they own Eradication Age and a bunch of weird, vague patents, like *a search function on a website with a blue search button.* That's one of them. Then they sue websites that step in their trap by doing something normal."

"Wait, do they, by chance have the rights to Robert Frost's poetry?"

"No, that doesn't make any sense, Oscar. They're patent trolls. And 2401 is owned by a company called Gonzago's Better Mousetrap Co. They don't make mousetraps, though.

They don't make anything, they're just metatrolls, and collect multiple patent troll firms and control their patents. 2401 is only part of their corporate suite. But this is where it gets really interesting. Because Gonzago's is owned in turn by a manufacturer of leather ballet equipment called Tutu Solid Flesh."

"Ew."

"But you see the pattern."

Since *Gonzago's Mousetrap Co.* and *Tutu Solid Flesh* were both garbled quotes from *Hamlet* (ca. 1600), Oscar at first thought that he could see the pattern; but then he decided that two examples were too few to establish a pattern and he said as much.

"What are you talking about?" Peters asked. "I mean that the ballet company is owned by—oh, hang on, it's my boss." Peters's cell phone was buzzing and she clicked it on. There followed a fragmented conversation within a conversation as Oscar waited patiently by. "What?...No, I said it rose in the east....I know the sun doesn't move; I meant it looks like it rises....Everyone says *it rises,* that's obviously what I meant....No, of course the sun doesn't go around the earth, that's not...okay, I'll be right there." She put the phone away, and said to Oscar, "That was my boss. I guess someone called him and said that a *Post* reporter claimed on record that the sun, well, you get the idea. I've got to hit the office and straighten everything out. Don't do anything stupid." And with that she was gone.

Oscar very casually moseyed over to Angie and told her that Peters got called away on a big scoop, and then moseyed further and sat with V.K. and Schwartz and because it was a three-seater he was sitting next to Schwartz, but then he was also sitting next to V.K., when he didn't want to be sitting next to anyone.

V.K. was telling a joke he had just made up, which Schwartz didn't understand at all.

Q.: How are what-dreams-may-come like a handshaking dog?

A.: They both must give us paws.

"Wait!" said Oscar. "Did you hear our conversation, the one between Peters and me?"

"Peters and I," corrected Schwartz.

"No, why?" said V.K.

So it went on. Oscar was lost in thought. What did he even eat? (*A*: Grilled chicken.)

They left and walked along Ditmars Avenue. Suddenly Schwartz broke into a run. "Look, damn it! there's a baby in the car!"

"Schwartz, no—"

"And the window's rolled up. It's July! That thing's going to boil."

"No, no, Schwartz—"

"I don't care if it is at night; it's July! Somebody get a photo of the license plate. I'm going to find a brick to break open that glass."

"No, no—"

But while Schwartz looked around for a brick, the light turned green, and the car with the baby in it, safe behind glass, drove away.

"Oh, Schwartz."

He was standing there with a brickbat, breathing heavily, the righteous indignation still throbbing in his veins.

"I just remembered," Oscar said. "I have to go to the City."

Which he did. But what was there to learn from a darkened and by all signs abandoned apartment far from the subway on the streets of Hell's Kitchen? There was a tiny brass plaque by the door of 451 W 55th Street, *Eradication Age, Inc.* There were apartments on the floors above, their windows illuminated, in the gathering dark, by the cold blue light of a cold blue medium. Nothing to see here.

Ah, but next door there was a scaffolding. There was a scaffolding next door.

· 13 · If you can't take the kitsch, stay out of the kitschen · Schopenhauerian planning · The point of entry · Oscar ascends a staircase partway · Keep your pants like your chin: up · Roofline · His fishing expedition · An envelope justifies all this strife ·

V.K. Kunti left for the library (as was his wont) the next morning, but Oscar did not go with him (as he often did). Perhaps Oscar Cox was going to spend his Thursday puttering around the apartment. Perhaps he was going to clean up the mildew in the shower—certainly the bottle of Mildon't–brand mildew remover "with bleach and other active agents" that he had left, conspicuously, out implied such a deed. But look—he has hidden the messenger bag and gun under the bed. He has put on jeans and a white T-shirt and a baseball cap. You wouldn't know this, necessarily, but that is not how he usually dressed. A flashlight on his belt, and now a mass-market paperback of Walter Scott's *The Fortunes of Nigel* (1822) just fitted in the back pocket.

Oscar Cox was Hell's Kitchen-bound on the BMT—as he always referred to this part of the subway, when he had a chance, so that casual listeners would assume he was a lifelong

New Yorker. What he did not have was a plan: just a series of potentialities; but sometimes potentialities were all you knew about, ahead of time. What were they, and by *they* he meant *we*, doing on the building next door? If construction workers were in the building, if Oscar Cox could get into the building, well perhaps he could get next to the offices of Eradication Age, Inc., and break through the wall with a...crowbar or something. Something might come up.

Schopenhauer (was it Schopenhauer?) claimed that life was a tragedy because you start out with an infinitude of possibilities and every decision you make cuts you off from more and more of them so that existence is nothing less than a constant autoëmasculation of your potential. John Greenleaf Whittier, who apparently was no longer one of the must-read poets among English students, assented: "For of all sad words of tongue or pen, / The saddest are these: 'It might have been!'" But this was hardly true in a heist! In a heist of potentialities, there were too many possibilities and not enough information to make a plan. Perhaps there are a billion billion potential Schrodinger's plans platonically floating around somewhere—unwieldily. But every moment brings new information and new information discards potential plan after plan until the billions are whittled down to a manageable amount, and then at last you can act! Oscar strode through Hell's Kitchen with only the dimmest idea not only of his methods but also of his goals.

It was a beautiful summer's morning. The rats were sunbathing; the pigeons were eating cigarette butts. People on stoops were reading the latest potboiler, some dimwitted plagiarism of a best seller from twenty years earlier. The avenues were crowded with restaurants: Thai Food Mary's; Pho Dive; General Tsonewall Jackson's Southern Fried Sweet

76

and Sour Chicken Emporium. Everything was a reference to something else. Everything was a groaner.

At the newsstands, *The Daily News* front page bore the head-line: "Dopernicus" and the subheadline: "*Post* Reporter Says Sun Goes Around Earth!" which was a little weird. The *New York Times* had it beneath the fold, but Oscar had peeked, and there it was: "Widely Maintained Heliocentric Theory Questioned by Ignorant Journalist, *Post*."

"Are you going to buy a Lotto ticket or what?" the news vendor asked, and Oscar put the paper down unread and scurried away to 451.

451 W 55th Street, home of E.A., Inc. There was something strange about Eradication Age. Beyond the name. There was little to distinguish its headquarters here from a normal apartment, ground floor front, with bars on the windows, unless you looked through the building's front door (via three small square windows, placed in a zigzag pattern) to its grungy tiled hallway. The door that would lead to Eradication Age was closed and most solidly padlocked, in a way apartment front doors rarely are. Even when apartment doors are most solidly padlocked, they are never this most solidly padlocked. Even the ones you think are. It was a lot of padlocks.

Oscar squinted through the office's barred front window, the one facing the street. It was dark in there, but when he placed his flashlight directly against the greasy, smudged glass he could see...that heavy dark curtains obscured the room. The curtains were not quite long enough, though, and peeping under the curtains, Oscar beheld primarily a thick layer of dust on the windowsill and beyond that several USPS sacks, incongruously clean and new, stacked and spilling mail out onto the bare and dusty floor.

Obviously Oscar did not take a moment to "get into character." He walked directly from 451 W 55 Street to 449 W 55 Street—some ten feet—and went under the scaffolding and through the open front door. Burlier men than he were carrying boards and buckets. Oscar picked up some boards and buckets and started carrying them around too.

"Hey," yelled a man. Did he have a clipboard? He had a clipboard. He also had a mouth like a crossword puzzle featuring very short words. His brow was furrowed. Perhaps the clues were too difficult. He did not look happy about the situation. "Where have you been?" he wanted to know.

"Smoking," said Oscar.

The man looked at Oscar long and hard. The way our hero stood, with all the weight on one hip—this was right. But something perhaps was wrong. The man stuck his hand out.

Oscar took it. And in a series of smooth complications, Oscar performed the secret grip. He was in the Union, after all.

"All right, fine," said the clipboard man, plopping a spare hardhat on Oscar's head. "Take some x to the y and z it onto the w."

Oscar did not know what any of these words meant, but he grunted assent and then, in an inspired moment, added, "Just let me drop these off first." He started up the stairs. The hardhat, he knew, had been his only missing piece. Now his disguise was perfect.

At the first landing, a man, burly, intercepted our hero. "Did Joe send you?" he asked.

"Joe who?" said Oscar.

"Joe Longman. Who else?"

"Just checking," said Oscar. "Yeah."

"Good. Drop those there and give me a hand with this."

The antecedent of *this* proved to be a very long series of actions involving carrying extremely heavy things, like bathtubs or toilets that were attached to...other toilets? for short to medium distances down a dusty and only half-renovated hall and into various apartments with no doors. Asbestos, like cotton candy, dangled from the sagging ceiling.

"Hold this."

"Take this over there."

"Turn this. No, turn it hard. Harder. I said *turn* it."

It was unpleasant. And Oscar realized something. He realized why men of action, like plumbers, sure, but also like construction workers and probably cowboys, always sported pants on a voyage halfway down their buttocks, buttcracks displayed. It turns out that there is a small part of one's brain that concentrates on keeping one's pants from slipping down. As we walk down the street, chat with friends, throw peanuts at squirrels, all the time we are concentrating, without even being aware, on the pants problem. *Don't let those pants fall down*, whispers this part of the brain, and our hips shimmy as we walk, and the pants stay in place.

But as soon as you carry a bathtub down a hallway, 100% of your brain is focused on the problem of how not to be crushed by a bathtub. There is no time for the pants. Oh, Oscar had focused hard on something before, such as a tricky word problem or a chess move, or even not drowning, but when had he ever focused hard on something *while standing up*? It was a dangerous world, the physical world, and there was no way to deal with it while your pants remained at full mast.

He also realized his muscles were about to give out and he would die. While something that may have been a cast-iron alien radiator was halfway down the hall he pretended he had a cell phone and pretended he had received a call. He used his wallet to pretend. "Oh, it's Joe Longman," he said, covering up the changepurse like a mouthpiece.

"Joe doesn't know how to use a pho—"

"I mean it's Mr. Pizzoli calling about Joe Longman. I've got to run for a moment. Be right back."

He went to the stairwell and ran up the stairs as fast as the lactic acid pooling in his legs would allow. He came out, forty feet up, on a roof that connected to 451's roof—just a hop over a knee-high wall—and he wandered around looking for a way down into 451, but the door on that roof was locked. There was scaffolding against 449, of course, but it looked rickety and ill-designed, and it was unclear anyway how he could make use of it. Over here, though, between the buildings, were two air shafts, maybe two-foot square each, shaded by little metal roofs on pegs, like chimney caps. The roofs came off easily, and Oscar considered for a moment trying to lower himself down, but chimneying along a four-story air shaft was more the kind of thing Oscar would claim he'd done than the kind of thing Oscar could actually do. He looked down one shaft, counting windows, and then wandered around again, snooping, until someone came up and asked him what he was up to up on the roof.

"Smoking," said Oscar, and headed downstairs. Schopenhauer was closing in, but perhaps Oscar had a plan. He went back down to the second floor, where that same burly man was trying to drag lengths of pipe from one apartment to another on his own.

"Thank God you're back," said the man from behind four inches of buttcrack.

"Yeah," said Oscar, but now he added the magic words. "I'm

supposed to tell you it's break time."

What was the guy going to say? "No, it's not break time"? "I insist that I continue to work"?

"You're allowed to smoke on the roof," Oscar added.

And now that he had the second floor to himself, Oscar grabbed three things. One was a twenty-five-pound hand-cranked drain augur. One was a paint-spattered tray of putty. One was a broom.

Obviously Oscar had no idea what a drain auger was for, or what drains people were planning on augering with this one. Only reason he knew it was a drain auger was because it said so on the side—if you had asked Oscar the day before what a drain auger was he would have heard *drain augur* and guessed "a Roman mystic who told the future by the eddies in a sewer; a copromancer." But now it was clear—a drain augur is like a gigantic plumber's snake, with a coil of cable on a spindle you can crank forward and back. And Oscar was lugging all twenty-five pounds of it into the second-floor front apartment, the apartment that bordered 451. He half dragged it, leaving a skid-trail in the plaster powder that coated the floor, to the bathroom. He closed and locked the bathroom door behind him.

Here is the thing: These old buildings were one up against the next, with no space between, of course; but that meant that the bathrooms would (in the days before electric fans rigged up to light switches) have been windowless miasmic stench chambers. And so the architect sunk air shafts, providing the bathrooms with an artificial exterior window to let the vile byproducts of human existence escape.

Naturally, no pooper wants to gaze from the toilet out a window across a two-foot space and through another window at his next-door neighbor as she also poops on the toilet. That was why there were two separate shafts: The bathrooms were staggered. In 451 the bottom-floor apartment had a bathroom over towards the front, close to the street, while the bottom-floor apartment of 449 had a bathroom in the middle of the building. Reverse for the second floor. The third-floor layout was like the first, fourth floor like the second. (This all only applies to the front apartments; there were presumably other shafts for the rear apartments.)

There in the shaft on the second floor, Oscar was looking down and across at the window that led to Eradication Age's bathroom. It was ten feet below him. More precisely it was the distance of the hypotenuse of a triangle with height of ten feet and base of two feet, but Oscar was not foolish enough to calculate that. The window was closed, and Oscar assumed he'd have to break it, so he leaned out the window very far and stretched out the broom handle. At the bottom of the shaft, where the unaugered drain had become choked with leaves, condoms, and candy wrappers, puddles bubbling with mosquito larva unleashed their bloodsucking air forces, and as the cloud of them enveloped his pan he almost bobbled his grip on the broom's straw bristles; but he caught himself and poked forward at the pane, and when the broom handle tapped the lower window it squeaked open.

Lucky break; nothing gets broken.

Then Oscar uncranked a length of drain auger and fastened some gummy putty to the end of the cable. With the help of the broom he shepherded the cable down the radical parenthesis two squared plus ten squared close parenthesis feet to the open first-floor bathroom window. Suicidal mosquitoes got themselves tangled in the putty. And when it was through the window he began to uncrank more, sending the cable snaking through the bathroom. The first attempt was a complete failure, and the sticky putty skidded to a halt against the bathroom floor, so the lengthening cable just fell in coils around it, but Oscar reeled in the cable, discarded the blacked and tiny-hair-encrusted putty, and applied new putty not all around the end of the cable, like a knob, but just on the top part, angled forward like a cap's brim. It took a couple of tries and a few dozen mosquito bites before Oscar got the cable to land on the bathroom floor correctly. He uncoiled more and more with the hand crank, and it took several more tries for him to find the bathroom door, which to be fair he could not see, and send the snake into the apartment. And then he would reel in, to find, like an unlucky angler, nothing but filthy putty, which he tossed saltily over his shoulder. No gold doubloons. No mirror-image comic strips. No *clues*. Nothing. Just the wet sound of putty hitting a mirror or a plumbing fixture.

And here he was, standing in a room in which every surface had spent a hundred years coated in other people's fecal effluvia. For nothing.

Also, there was always the risk that...you know, that guy... would come back from his break. "What the devil are you doing there?" he'd say, and what would Oscar reply?

"Smoking"?

No, that would never do. Oscar cast again. The cable skittered into the darkness. The mosquitoes became more daring, and started flying up out of the shaft right through the window into Oscar's pan, which was full of his precious blood. To bat them away would mean several moments—several *cherished* moments—not groping blindly with a mechanical snake. He tried to bite them out of the air. Cast and cast again.

Say, angler! Are they biting?

[Snapping at mosquitoes] "What is the antecedent of *they*?"

And look! as he reeled the auger back in, there was something attached to the putty, something white that fell off just as it came into view, bumping up against the tub. Oscar took a moment to kill several squadrons of bloodsuckers, and then went back to his fishing. Now he had something he was actually fishing for, which was in fact far more difficult and frustrating. He cast and missed. He cast and missed.

The knob rattled.

"Occupied," Oscar called out automatically.

"What do you mean, 'occupied'? Nothing's hooked up."

"I'm—" Oscar started.

"You damn well better not be smoking in there."

"Almost done," said Oscar, who had snagged the white thing at last. It reeled into better sight—it was a paper—an envelope—

The knob rattled some more. "Almost done what?"

Look, I don't know if you've ever tried to drag an envelope stuck to putty up a wall and out a window and up and over ~10.2 feet to another window without dropping the envelope into the infested stagnant puddles below. Really, one thing you would not need, if you tried it, is an angry voice and a pounding at the door behind you. This took all of Oscar's concentration. There was a mosquito on his *eyeball*. His pants were practically down around his knees.

Perhaps this is not what happened, but this is what it looked like happened: The envelope, up and out the window, swinging on its pendulum string in the shaft, did it slip free and fall? Did it fall just as a new cloud of mosquitoes launched themselves upward from their watery base? Was it borne back aloft on the backs of a hundred tiny winged hematophages, high enough for Oscar to grab it out of the sky and stuff it down his shirt? No, no, that is not possible, probably Oscar used the broom: but the adrenaline and the way Oscar leaned out into a cloud of pinpricks—well, it *looked like* it happened that way.

The door was still banging, and it was not banging itself, so Oscar opened it. "I'm not going to lie to you," he said to a strange startled face. "I am a heroin addict. I know that I'm fired and I deserve it."

He handed the man his hard hat, which miraculously had not fallen off into the shaft. It was covered with the twisted carcasses of squashed mosquitoes. Everything about this is disgusting. Leaving behind only a footprint fragment in a filthy splotch of putty, Oscar hurried down the stairs past burly men, one of whom might be Joe, and out to the sidewalk. Two blocks away before he stopped in the shade of a Starbucks awning to extract the envelope and see what he'd acquired.

The envelope—blackened where it had dragged, and sticky with putty—was a USPS overnight flat-rate. It was print-stamped and addressed to Monica Dixon of Katonah, NY. She and a guest were invited to an "exclusive charity ball" in a "five star hotel" at 99 Fulton Street—this Sunday. That was in three days.

"Fulton Street, Fulton Street." Oscar racked his brains to remember where that was. He had a vague idea it was in the Bronx, near a fish market—but then he remembered: Fulton Street the subway station was in Manhattan. Over near the lack of a WTC, one block away from the Port Authority Trans Hudson train to the the New Jerusalem, down in the Financial District. Why would anyone ever go down to the Financial District?

Oscar would have to go down to the Financial District.

· 14 · A program in reading · The Masterson—Parker/Crockett—Hudson continuum · "Tekeli-li!" · A brief hint at dissatisfaction with the apparatus of public schooling · The hairpin turn to mathematics · The purpose of Labor · A program in reading, continued and now subsidized ·

"Let's talk more about that fascinating Oscar Cox!"...

...is a sentence that could be heard in two or three states now, uttered in hushed tones by the duly impressed.

"*I'm* not fooled," brags a jaded cynic, who is nonetheless fooled, because doubting 50% of Oscar's rodomontade means you are fooled, and doubting 100% of Oscar's rodomontade means you are still fooled, because 120% of the things he says are false. If you doubt the math, Oscar would have been glad (absent current restrictions) to whip up a few abstruse proofs that you may also doubt but which you will be unable to convincingly argue do not support these statistics.

Certainly Oscar Cox of the abstruse proofs was good at math. He had once been good at many things. The first thing he was good at was *school*, which is a relatively worthless thing to be good it; but it impresses the yokels. He added four and eight and usually got twelve at a very tender age. He read all the books in the kindergarten classroom, and then all the books in the school library—not literally, but he read a lot of them—and then he was reading his way through the public library, except it kept acquiring new books, so trying to read all of it was a little like the man who said he'd be able to swallow the sea provided someone stop all the rivers and streams from always pouring in and filling it up.

The first thing he'd had a passion for reading about was the cowboy. This is hardly unusual for a boy of certain age, when *cowboy* means not so much *a job* as a gun and a special outfit and a horse and the freedom to shoot the gun while riding the horse in the special outfit at whomever—parent, teacher, Indian Chief—you thélèmically please.

But the idea of being a cowboy, of suspending his youthful disbelief long enough to imagine a cowboy future, bumped up against the challenging fact that New Jersey was not exactly teeming in 1. range, 2.*a.* buffalo, *b.* antelope, 3. Indians, 4. lone prairie, or 5. even so many cows. So Oscar dialed his chronometer back a bit and started reading about frontiersmen of the Boone/Crockett school. At least Jersey (*pace* New Yorkers' popular belief) had trees. Jersey had a Delaware Water Gap. Very scenic, garden state.

Of course, woods are a far cry from the forest primeval where Fess Parker, 6'5" of natural man, blazed his trails for elbow room. WPIX channel 11 showed his syndicated adventures in *Daniel Boone* (1964–70) every morning at some ungodly hour—6 AM maybe—during the more impressionable periods of Oscar's youth—and Fess's Daniel never once seemed to be striding across New Jersey. In fact Boone-Town, NJ (1761), was named after...(wait for it)...Thomas Boone, who was not even a frontiersman but rather a Colonial Governor who so obstructed the Jersey legislature with his dictatorial decrees that the state government fell apart and only reassembled itself when Gov. Boone ignominiously slunk back to England.

"East of the Mississippi" as he was, what awaited Oscar but civilization—Knickerbockers to the north, Quakers to the south—and what was a young frontiersman to do in these parts?

So in direct contravention of all reality principles, young Oscar dialed his chronometer back further, to become an explorer in days before states were united, or even were colonies. He read books about the Verrazzano days, the Henry Hudson days, when Elizabeth Hoboken and Trenton Palisades stalked the land, naming everything they could find after themselves.

You may suspect that it would have been difficult to persuade the other kids to play at the explorations of Giovanni da Verrazzzanno, a man so obscure his namesake Verrazano Bridge spells him wrong, but exploration (16th –17th centuries) is so fraught with dangers, massacres, wild beasts, wild men, mutinies, starvation, and cataclysm that any red-blooded American youth would jump at the chance to pretend to die in the wilderness, his corpse feasted upon by pumas. Those happy golden days! At the library, one particular Dewey decimal had Oscar's boyish footprints worn deep in the carpet (not literally. I mean, it's not like he was just standing there scuffing his feet or marching in place for hours. He took the books home) before it.

But eventually reality, long suppressed, slithers to the top like a Freudian nightmare, and Oscar realized that he would not be able to explore the coast of New Jersey, which was metaphorically overrun by beasts and wild men once again but more literally was just a bunch of skeeball jernts. Frontiers were one natural resource that the USA was not exactly abounding in in the '80s.

Alaska billed itself as if not the final then at least the last frontier, but every statement on a license plate smacks of marketing (do you really have a friend in Pennsylvania?), and perhaps there was further to go...miles even.

And so Oscar changed his reading to cover the polar explorers: either Pole: two Poles, no waiting: John Franklin, Ernest Shackleton, Peter Freuchen. Walrus-fighting, cannibalism, and death (not respectively). The search for a Pole was, by standard metaphor, the search for an unchanging truth, one of the dizzy Earth's only two fixed points. This made these inaccessible reaches (reached and accessed before Oscar Cox was born, of course) more than just cartographic trivia for map wonks. Poe, Verne, and Lovecraft—a kind of triple muse for a certain kind of boy—offered dark hints of what might be found in the polar recesses. A white giant, a sphinx of ice, things *much worse.*

Freuchen once, when trapped inside a walled-up ice cave in Greenland sans equipment, froze his own poop and crafted it into a dagger to chip his way out. This is hard to beat for a ten-year old boy, even one like Oscar. He spent a long time debating with himself. If the poop was *frozen,* surely it wouldn't be so *bad.* In the end, though, it was not the poop that scared him off, it was the fact that he hated the cold. "Well, I bet Robert Falcon Scott hated scurvy, and that didn't stop him." Yes, but Scott died with all his men in the second-to-last leg of a long cold losing race. By this point, though, Oscar was old enough to understand that he would not be "conquering" the already-subjugated Poles. He could indulge in a monomania for its own sake. And so he bundled himself in an electric blanket or he sat directly on the heating grate in the kitchen floor and read about *the time north of the Arctic circle that one member of Franklin's starving party began killing and eating, one by one, the others, and because he was the only one who had tasted protein in weeks no one else was strong enough to hinder him.*

By force of law, a child's interests must be fed through, as all juvenile things must be fed through, the panoptic moloch of his school day. When it was time for a book report, Oscar read, if not Verne etc., then Shackleton's simply named *South.* (Jack

89

London in a pinch; at least it was Arctic.) When it was time for a social studies report—countries of the world—Oscar trotted out the disputed British Antarctic territory of Enderby Land. In science class, ice calving, polar bears, prehistoric antarctic amphibian fossils, the sufferings of 1. fuel, 2. machinery, or 3. flesh at 200° Kelvin, or *something like that* could be coaxed onto stage at every opportunity. Weary teachers' eyes had begun to glaze over by sixth grade. By junior high, the fact that Oscar had managed to read a book as thick (640 pages) and old (1922) as Apsley Cherry-Garrard's *Worst Journey in the World* was simply sufficient evidence that Oscar deserved a good grade. There was no need to actually peruse his lengthy analysis of how to steal a penguin egg or why who ate which dog when. A. A–. A. They had snow blindness.

Insofar as the only goal of school is to get good grades, Oscar was, you know, *winning*. But the glazed look on Miss Grundy's pan as she scrawled an arbitrary mark across "A Potential Network of Canals to Create a True Northwest Passage" by Oscar J. Cox was too obvious. The notes he left mid-paragraph on page three—"Let me know if you see this"; "Miss Grundy resembles Mr. Ed"; "I am literally going to blow up the school and murder everyone in it like tomorrow this is no joke but a terrible cry for help help soon you will die oh well"—got no response. And here you see the problem.

You may argue it didn't actually matter what the teachers thought of Oscar's papers and book reports, and you'd be right. But if you are good at school (as Oscar was), presumably you are good at learning lessons, and while it turns out there are several lessons school is designed to teach you, I guarantee that The Opinions of Teachers Do Not Matter is not one of them.

"Screw this," said young Oscar, age (by this point) fourteen or so. "I'll become good at math." Math tests were *always read over*. Sure, they could be graded by a robot or a teaching assistant, but never would it be said that a math problem didn't *count*, that a math problem could pass unseen over a desk and back to Oscar's folder with a fake grade on it.

Naturally, this plan would only work if Oscar had already been good at math. Perhaps Oscar's math grade did not even increase after his decision. But Oscar changed himself from "the polar guy" to "the math guy." This was when he started memorizing the numbers of steps, in the hopes of passing himself off as an autistic human calculator and world's wonder. Perhaps someday he'd be able to casually drop some information—"As you know, there are twenty-three steps between the first and second floors of out high school"—but, no. This plan did not pan out. He also counted how many toothpicks were in the never-used family toothpick box in the cupboard, so that in case anyone ever spilled it he could say, instantly, "500." But it never came up. Even when he balanced the box precariously on the shelf's edge, no one knocked it off.

But he also memorized various mathematical tricks and shortcuts for multiplying large numbers or summing long series, and these were easier to massage into conversations. "Did you say you wanted to find the square root of 729?"

His most glorious moment—a stroke of luck he pounced upon, for strokes are like gazelles, and this is what you must do if you would be a lion—came his sophomore year. It happened that Oscar had a gastropodic sad sack of a friend—this was Willie Verge—who had been born on a Friday the 13th and obsessively blamed all his woes, David Copperfield-style, on this natal misfortune. One February 13th in 1992, a girl in Oscar's home room mentioned to her seatmate that it was her birthday. It also happened that this (Oscar knew) was Willie Verge's birthday, and, assuming, safely, that Willie and the girl were the same age, Oscar pretended, there in homeroom, to spend two or three seconds in mental calculation. "That means," said Oscar to the girl, "that you must have been born on a Friday. A Friday the 13th."

"Holy crap," said the girl.

And word of such a mental calculation, spontaneous and un-fakeable, made the rounds. After that Oscar was most definitely the math guy, and he remained the math guy throughout high school and he was, if known for other things, nevertheless academically the math guy at A—t, and what could stop him from continuing to be a math guy in New York, except perhaps a T.A. strike?

Because this strike dragged on and on, eighteen months now. The iron was no longer hot, clearly, and yet they struck on. Bear in mind that the Union is supposed to keep you from starving to death while you are on strike. That is part of the purpose of a union. But it doesn't want to just send you free money. Perhaps you would be required to walk a picket line or inflate a giant rubber rat (take care inflating, for those suckers are pricey: $3500 for a twelve-foot version, item #78331A in the Standard Novelty Inc. Catalog Special Edition for Labor). Perhaps you would just be requested to get another, crummier, job, temporarily.

There was no picket line at the moment, at least none at N—Y— University; possibly because it would have interfered with construction. There was no giant inflatable rat, either. Frankly, this close to Washington Square, a giant rat would have been redundant; and, what was worse, another union on another strike had learned that setting a giant rat up round here simply attracted herds, or more properly *tides* of closer-to-normal-sized rats, who would seek to mate with it, and, when that failed, to eat it. The first rat bite into its rubber hide—you can imagine the pop, the terror as the rat tide ebbed from the hissing gradual death of their twelve-foot rat god. $3500 of flaccid rubber.

"Deflater mouse," V.K. Kunti said when he heard about it, which is unfair, since they were not mice but rats, but at least it establishes that he knew something about the nineteenth-century German classical tradition, which may prove relevant later.

So there would be no reenactment of the Platonic ideal of striking; there would be no long hard days at the picket/rat-mongering line. Oscar would have to go and get a job; but please note the problem. He could not be a cashier. Cashiers must do math. He could not be a stock boy. Stock boys do math.

Is punching numbers into a cash register not *math*?

Well, um, lessee, um...

And if not, then why should punching numbers into a calculator be *math*?

Erm, well, you see, hmmmm...

And so a good half of the menial jobs were out. Janitorial work was out, because cleaning staffs had their own union, and Oscar was strictly forbidden to join a secondary union (the God-and-Mammon clause of his Union oath). Food service work was out, because Oscar failed the government-mandated food-handling exam (perhaps he was not really trying). There were plenty of places that would illegally waive this requirement, but Oscar was insufficiently fluent in Spanish and/or Chinese for them to accept him. By this point, Oscar was simply gleefully failing every job requirement the Union demanded he try. He failed to get a Class-B motor-vehicle license. He failed the realtor

93

exam. He failed the not-allergic-to-dogs requirement, the only requirement, really, for becoming an assistant inseminator at the Happy Puppy Mill bitchery. Man, did he break a lot of dishes the first day he washed any. He figured that if he could just wear them down, they'd let him go back to being a mathematics grad student, which was, you understand, what he'd been trying to be in the first place.

But you do not wear down a union. In Soviet Russia, perhaps, you wear down a union, but that is not what happens here. There were construction workers, of various stripes, all over town, and since they were part of the Union, they would take Oscar if the Union requested it.

Oscar went down to the construction site. He learned that the man with the clipboard was in charge. He learned that everyone wore a hardhat. He learned the cocked-hipped way they stood.

That was pretty much all he learned. The thing about construction work is that even more than dishwashing it is a skilled job, and skills were what Oscar lacked. There was no point even letting him try out the pneumatic drill, when mayhem and massacre would be the inevitable. So they had Oscar stand around idly. After a few hours (actually: about forty-five seconds) of idle standing, Oscar would pull out a book, and soon he'd be sitting, off to one side nose-deep, while skilled men strained their muscles nearby. The sight of a Union worker sitting on an eight-hour coffee break was too much for scabs, rats, goons, ginks, company finks, and assorted dissatisfactoria to stand, so the word came down that Oscar was not to read books while standing less-obviously idly for eight hours.

"Well, okay," said Oscar, "but it's just that when my brain is not focusing on something, sometimes it wanders to the things it used to think about. Things like—"

Don't say math.

"—math."

Well, stop it then.

"It's a totally unconscious process."

Do not let your unconscious mind think about math.

"But it happens automatically."

Think about something else. Think about boobs.

"But what if I think of two ladies, and then there are 2X2=4 boobs?"

Don't think about that, for heaven's sake! Think about something else. What do people think about when they're trying to prevent their brains for thinking about something?

"Sheep, usually."

Yes, sheep!

"So you're saying I should count sheep?"

Aaaaaaa!

And so there was a new plan, and Oscar was forbidden to hang out, idly, at construction sites, although he was still on the payroll and still got his checks from Rrida Construction Inc.

(That was not the actual name of the construction company. That was just what V.K. called them.)

Since Oscar was still a student—a student forbidden to work in his field of study—Oscar had access to N— Y— University's Rufus Library, and there he would sit, hour after hour, learning more and more about the wrong books. Agnes Repplier. Thomas Love Peacock. Edgar Saltus. No math here. He found himself able to bluff his way through any conversation with V.K.'s peers as long as it didn't involve intradepartmental politics. When he hadn't read the book, he had read the Cliff's Notes—and he had read a lot of Cliff's Notes—but now that the Union/Rrida was paying him to sit in Rufus Library with his feet up all day, he needed less and less to rely on these trots. "Trots are for Trotskyites."

It seemed a fine life, but of course there would be trouble ahoy. His grants and stipends and scholarships would eventually expire. It would be hard to apply for new ones when his foremost accomplishment over the years had been doing less math than the average wrestling referee (which is a low bar; at least boxing refs count to *ten*). At any moment gay marriage could be legalized. Also, Oscar had to kill someone *or else*, and a shadowy Russian Doll of weird companies had accidentally invited him to what might turn out to be, after all, a snuff brothel in of all places *the Financial District*. There he was, on the long walk back from Hell's Kitchen to the subway beneath the merciless noonday sun, and with nothing but a long day of worry ahead.

"I would it were bed-time, Hal, and all well."

Not yet, old man.

· 15 · Just immanentize it! · Vera ahoy · Let him on · Memorial · Our hero looks for more clues, interviews someone who is not a Prussian admiral · They pt. 1 · The catalog of agnosis ·

Oscar Cox had arrived in New York in 1998, and already the air had been pre-apocalyptic. People were afraid that a computer bug would, in two years, melt down civilization. People were afraid that the millennium would usher in the Rapture and the End of Days. People were afraid that other people might celebrate the millennium in the wrong year. People were afraid of everything except the right thing, and then 2001 came along and the Chicken Littles had the sky fall on their heads for real and no one was prepared. Mayor Giuliani took off his dress and grabbed a bullhorn and said it was not the apocalypse, but no one was falling for that one again.

Oscar remembered (*never forget!*) 9/11, and he remembered the confusion afterwards about what to call what happened. For a pseudo-Checkuary of like three weeks, people called it "the bombing" before correcting themselves. Bombings were what they were kind of expecting. No one knew what to say. "The attack" seemed too jingoistic. "The WTC" seemed too Pentagonless. "The incident" seemed too bureaucratese. After the fall of the Tower of Babel people had had the same problem, so this was not without precedent. But it was unprecedented in Oscar's lifetime. "Where were you during the bombing...er...I mean the thing that happened last week, you know?"

The unhappy neologism 9/11 crept up *faute de mieux*. And the ax of a second apocalypse seemed, like everything else, about to come down.

That was the autumn that Cinnamon Crispies had their unfortunate commercial jingle:

> Cinnamon, where you gonna run to,
> Cinnamon, where you gonna run to,
> Cinnamon, where you gonna run to,
> All on that day?

(The idea was that the Cinnamon Crispies mascot could not escape from the children who wanted to eat his cereal, even if he ran to the rock, the sea, etc.) Also the autumn of Eschatonic Water, another failed brand ("make an end to thirst"). The autumn Oscar got engaged for the second round. Poor Vera

Rodriguez came to see him one last time, to wish him congratulations and tell him she was essentially running away to sea, only it wasn't so irresponsible since she was, after all, studying marine biology. Oscar would almost have felt guilty about his lies and his unfairnesses, except he'd recently read in Edmund Wilson's *Classics and Commercials* (1950) that in order to escape an engagement, Kafka deliberately caught tuberculosis, so Oscar's fibs seemed comparatively like fine ideas. Also, now he was lying to and being unfair to a new patsy. So there was that. Here was another potential apocalypse always waiting in the wings. It all fit together.

And, indeed, the sense of apocalypse seemed so acute at all times that it hardly surprised Oscar, as he stood on the crowded A train heading from Hell's Kitchen to Fulton Street, when an old man at the 34th Street stop kept shouting, as he tried to board, "Armageddon! Armageddon!"

Only after the masses on the car had redistributed themselves and the man had squeezed in did Oscar realize that he had actually been saying, vernacularly, "I'm-a get on."

Down on Fulton Street, Oscar rode the exiting tide out of the car and walked past the so-called "ground zero" to the so-called "five-star hotel," as listed on Monica Dixon's invite. It looked pretty swank. The imitation gold on the door's trimmings, the massive foyer with its potted palms, glimpsed, if dimly, through tinted doors governed by a doorman with epaulets like a Prussian admiral.

The New York rule is that no matter how many stars your hotel or restaurant, the filthy, blood-spattered sidewalk outside is only like one, one-and-a-half stars tops. There was indeed an old man—there was always an old man—possibly crazy, in a sidewalk beach chair right outside the hotel entrance. He was reading the new potboiler. An ancient cane was crooked on his arm. *But even he was wearing a tuxedo.* This place was class.

Oscar, his hair dusty from the construction gig and his face a slowly deflating morass of insect bites, suspected he would have to do a lot of fast talking to make it through the door, and he might want to save some of that for later, as this was merely a scouting expedition. Let's go talk to the crazy old man in the lawn chair first.

"So," Oscar said, sidling up next to the tuxedo. "What's going down?"

"You with the charity ball?" the man asked, setting his book on a plastic armrest. His hair, unlike most people's, was white and/or missing. The combination of a prognathous jaw and a bulging forehead gave him a pan that kindness might call moon-shaped, but which Oscar thought looked like it had been stepped on in the middle.

"I'm going to the ball on Sunday," Oscar said, suddenly feeling Cinderellish.

"You think it's going to be here, too?"

"Is it uncertain? I thought the invite said this address for sure."

The old man almost jumped out of his chair, except he was too old. "You got your invite already?"

Oscar said quickly but smoothly, "I'm a premium member."

"I thought sure they weren't going out till tomorrow."

And here Oscar thought about the envelope, safely tucked under his shirt. Overnight delivery. Going out Friday, say, for Saturday delivery, and the ball is the day after. "How'd you know it was here, then?"

"I wasn't certain, but there were signs and clues. Portents. See that address, 99? It's not one hundred, is it? And you know what one hundred has that none of the numbers one through 99 have?"

"Three digits?" guessed Oscar.

"I can see you're not one for math," said the old man. "It has a *d*. No smaller number has the letter *d* in it, not till one hundred. Every other letter in *hundred* is in a smaller number: *h* is in *three*, *u* is in *four*"—the old man went through them all, the *n* and the *r* and the *e*, but we'll leave the proof to the reader. "But not," he continued, "*d*. No *d*; 99 has no *d*."

"No *d*," said Oscar.

"*Nod*. It spells Nod, the land Cain was exiled into. Get it? Just as we poor wanderers are exiles from our true spiritual home. All the pieces fit. Signs and portents. I thought I had at least a thirty percent chance of getting it right, so it was worth the attempt."

"The attempt?"

"To see them when they set up. So see if *they* come." He pronounced the word *they* strangely, but only the once. Otherwise it was normal.

"What kind of delio is this going to be anyway?" Oscar asked, acting casual. "I've never been before."

"How'd you get to be a premium member if you've never been?"

"Grandfathered in. My uncle bought it for me as a late birthday present."

"I honestly didn't even know there were premium memberships."

"So. The delio."

The old man's eyes—I apologize, but this is literally true—twinkled as he leaned forward. "Oh, you will be delighted, young man. You will be enlightened. There'll be some networking, and a little light multi-level marketing, of course. But there are also gurus available, and there is the hope that *they* might come, or at least a representative." That strange, hissing mispronunciation again.

"That does sound enlightening."

"I shouldn't say too much, you're better off going in cold. It's not good to be too prepared for some things, it hampers the experience. Let's just say: If it goes well, it should be worth the sticker price. This will be my third—they don't happen very often you, know, and I have to save up to afford it."

"How much did my Uncle Pud blow on this ticket?" Oscar asked.

"It probably depends on his broker, but this is going to set me back seventy grand."

"*Dollars?*"

"I don't know how much a premium membership is worth."

Oscar was feeling guilty about Monica Dixon and her life savings gone with no golden ticket to show. But after all, this was a matter of etc. Surely Monica would understand. Oscar nodded, sagely, because he'd stopped paying attention for a moment but he knew sage nodding was always an acceptable maneuver. "And you're here lining up early, like a *Star Wars* fan, or..."

"I just want a glimpse of one. Before the masks are on, you know. When *they*'re not expecting it."

"Right, right. And just to remind me. Who are they?

"*They*," he corrected. "Oh, don't you know? *They* are the ones who control the Rothschilds."

"Right, the Rothschilds."

"And the Rotary Club and the Rosicrucians. All of them. Do you know the Hittite Story?"

Oscar looked around. There was so much, of course, he didn't know. He didn't know if *an address stolen from another address gleaned from a firearm registration* was a clue or just a dumb coincidence. He didn't know how he was going to find 1. M. "Scrote" Johnson and 2. a way not to kill M. "Scrote" Johnson. He didn't even know if there really were Prussian admirals, or what their epaulets looked like. (*Answer*: yes to the Prussian admiral, but in all of history only one: Prince Heinrich Wilhelm Adalbert von Hohenzollern; epaulets: suitably huge; looked it up.)

Most of all, though, Oscar did not know the Hittite Story. So the old man told him the Hittite Story.

• 16 • The Hittite Story •

You know who the Hittites were?

More or less.

So: long ago, over 3000 years ago, in the waning days of the Hittite Empire, a Hittite official in the city of Hattusa was disgraced. Nobody knows his name, so let X stand for this unknown. X was charged with absconding with military supplies, a serious crime in those days, and got himself placed under interdict. In the Hittite Empire, *interdict* was the most terrible of punishments, and it lasted for seven generations. X, and his descendants, would be non-people, absolutely forbidden from decent society. Hittites in good standing could abuse, enslave, or even kill them with impunity. It was a real good joke, in those days, when good jokes were few: To hold an interdict down while a horse pooped on him. To stuff him down the hole in an outhouse. To wait till he was squatting on the side of the road (outhouses, like all buildings, were forbidden to interdicts) and push him over into his own pile of feces. Hittite humor was very scatological.

Interdict families usually just died off in a generation or two, because why would an interdict want to bring a child into the world only to have it hucked into the poop, and who would have sex with an interdict anyway? But X had seven children—some say seven sons, but maybe it was seven children, boys and girls—and he took them aside on the day of his disgrace. He must have told them that their lives of leisure were at an end, that this palatial cyclopean manor house with its god-carved walls and lapis lazuli filigree was going to be torn down—at great effort, to be sure—and scattered. Flung roses etc. But he also told them a family secret. He told them that each of them must have seven children, and each must adjure his or her seven children to have seven children in turn, with the same adjuration. And he also told them that he had arranged for his storehouses of treasure to be taken—from this, the manor house, and from his country houses on the Mediterranean coast—and buried in a secret cave in a secret location as a contingency against just such a circumstance. He would tell them where the cave was, and they must tell their children, etc., but of course they should not go dig it up, for they were interdicts, and it would simply be taken from them. But in the eighth generation (who would be free and clear), when the eldest of the eighth generation celebrated his fortieth birthday, all the Xids should gather at the cave and inherit their patrimony.

And so began a long slog of nightmarish lives and ignomin-ious deaths. The first few years were perhaps the worst, when X's fall from glory was so fresh in the mind that everybody in

Hattusa vied for the greatest poop jape upon him. X himself was finally suffocated, his head stuffed in an ox's rectum, which is not something an ox will usually stand for—but nobody liked X. His children had it little better, but they managed to perdure. They took as their spouses lowly and despised foreigners, Hattians and Yortans and the Lycian, Mysian, and Mæonian band, or escaped slaves or noseless grifters or even the secret troglodytic and possibly reptilian degenerated descendants of Çatal Höyük. They told their children, and their children mated with human garbage and told their children, and they were covered at all times with filth and sores and they slept in the rain and they told their children. Hope of a final redemption, of wealth and a phoenix-like shining name in this, the immortal Hittite Empire, kept them alive, and breeding. After a couple generations they didn't even need to go look for Yortans to mate with, for there were Xid second cousins, and then third cousins, and even if these things were forbidden to Hittites (debatable), the advantage to being an outlaw is that the law does not apply. Despicable deeds were done on the streets of Hattusa. And the generations passed.

For a century and a half, the people of Hattusa had a great joke at the expense of the crawling, sniveling Xids. But fair was fair. When the eighth generation came along, the Hittites didn't spit on them. They didn't poop on them. The didn't kill them and skin them and wear their skin, as some might fear. They pooped and spat with renewed vigor on their seventh-generation parents, of course, because this was going to be their final opportunity. The bar is closing, last call. And so the eighth generation grew up—poor and filthy, of course— but relatively free; and a constant witness to the humiliation of their parents. Their cheeks burned with shame, and they counted the days.

At last, the eldest of the eighth generation of Xids turned forty, which seemed an arbitrary number. He—we can let him be Y—had endured already a lifetime of shame, watching his mother ground to death beneath the wheel of a cart, his father fed to pigs, merciful ends to their miserable lives. There was poop involved too. For his birthday there would be no pinata and no party; he simply girded his loins, and headed out, outside the city limits. Word had spread, to all the scattered Xids throughout the Hittite Empire, Y's cousins and his second cousins and his other cousins, some of whom were also his uncles and aunts, and all the free eight generation gathered around him.

Not every Xid had had seven children, of course—it would have been a difficult order to follow even if you didn't need to scrounge for scraps like a rat. But many Xids had had seven children. And many more had had six, or five. There were hundred of Xids who gathered there that day around Y as he headed for the gates, and thousands who thronged around him as he strode away from the city. They all knew where to go. Triumph was burning in their eyes, for they too had seen their parents' degradation, and they longed to return bedecked in gold and jewels and show Hittite "society" that they, too, belonged in Mrs. Astor's ballroom. Perhaps some of them looked around them, at the tens of thousands of cousins milling about, and wondered: *How big could my cut possibly be?*

But now was not the time to worry about that. For Y had dug up the entrance. Y had rolled away the stone. From the cave came a glittering in the morning light. How the great the press must have been, and people pushed and jostled to see what Y had uncovered.

There in the cave, they saw, was no gold and no gems and no precious spices and not even any nard. Instead—behold, the treasure of the Xids!—there stood row upon row of iron axes and curved bronze swords and curved iron swords. They needed a polish, perhaps, but perhaps there was no time for a polish. Y passed them out to the Xid masses, tossing them like flower petals, like candy at the Memorial Day parade. Everyone had an ax or everyone had a sword, or possibly a spear or, for the little ones, a dagger, and how short a trip back to Hattusa it was, especially at a run.

And if the Hattusans barred the gates the Xids forced down the gates and if they hid in their manor houses the Xids tore down the manor houses. And the blood flowing through the streets washed clean the aged surviving seventh- and sixth-generation Xids, who danced for joy to finally be cleansed of so many decades of ordure and shame.

And that was the end of Hattusa, and that was the end, shortly after, of the Hittite Empire. But that was the start of *They*.

• 17 • **Walter t.b.c.** • **No sign of Peters** • *Lawrence v. Texas* • **An unsuccessful Jurassic quip** • **What kind of poetry does V.K. Kunti write, anyway? The answer** • **Does he only keep Oscar around because Oscar understands his jokes?** • **A lavatory triumph** •

Was there a beginning to all things? Does a bereshit in the woods?

If you were puzzled by the Hittite Story, you can join Oscar Cox, who at least had finally worked out that *They* was pronounced with a hissing *th*, as in *thin* or *theory*. The word was from a particular dialect of Hurrian, or possibly a related Indo-European language. Patience, foresight, endurance, vengeance, and bloodthirstiness—the virtues *They* embody—were there from the beginning. Planting the seed of a poisoned tree that blooms after a thousand years. *They* frequented balls, retreats, events, and openings such as this one in the hopes of recruiting the illuminated and the aware. *They* sought the "Mason Word," so-called...whatever that was.

The old man would not regiment Oscar's coming experience by explaining more. He did give his name—Walter Pilkoç—and a hearty handshake and a sincere wish to see Oscar again on Sunday. He also intimated that dress would be formal.

Because the man saying this was wearing a tux, Oscar did not say, "Formal like a button-down shirt or formal like with a tie, too?" as he ordinarily would have.

Oscar headed back to Astoria, which is quite a ways from Fulton Street. He should probably buy some groceries. He should probably straighten up the apartment, actually use the decoy mildew spray. Instead he worked on his plan until V.K. came home.

So V.K. entered and after a quick kiss Oscar suggested that he really had a hankering to go to Barb's for dinner.

"Again?"

Yes, again. Really, he just hoped Peters would be there for additional grilling, but dinner passed and she did not show. One man, a Serb, apparently, did approach Oscar about "pulling an Archduke Ferdinand" on some Swedish legislator Oscar had never (like every member of Sweden's Riksdag) heard of, but Oscar just told him he could only take one assignment at a time. And this, too, was an unpleasant reminder of what Oscar would have to do tomorrow.

107

"Crazies, am I right?" Oscar said when the man left.

"You handle them well," said V.K., who had seen Oscar semi-ironically pretend to be a mercenary or a sniper ("No more for me, I'm on call." "Oh, are you a doctor?" "Not exactly...") enough times that it hardly even seemed weird.

Afterwards Oscar and V.K. headed down Ditmars to the local bookstore, The Tome Machine. The front room was new releases—just pile after pile of that paranoid potboiler today—but it was the siren call of the used books stacked two-deep on each shelf in the back room that drew our heroes. Perhaps that is not correct, perhaps V.K. is not also our hero. Better: Our hero (an invite might say; this is not math) plus one.

A fellow Oscar did not know but who apparently was in V.K.'s program stopped and chatted them up in a tedious way about the Supreme Court and current events that everyone seemed to know more about than Oscar. He showed off the coffee table book he'd be purchasing, *Muhammad Ali's Greatest Hits* ("It's really violent!"), and then he asked about Saturday and every reference to the passage of time—yes, this, too, was another reminder that tomorrow Oscar was supposed to kill someone in cold blood and with no do-overs.

"What are you going be reading?" the man asked V.K. "Something from the Brontë Sisters?"

"Technically, I believe you mean the Apatosisters," V.K. said.

This was V.K.'s specialty, nineteenth-century women's fiction. Everyone assumed by this that he studied the big guns—Austen, Brontës, Eliot—but of course there was nothing left to study there and nothing new to say. V.K.'s master's thesis had been on Jane Louden née Webb's 1827 futuristic teenage melodrama *The Mummy!* (complete with exclamation point), with his doctoral dissertation focusing instead on the obsolete and ephemeral genre of temperance literature. Edmund Lester Pearson had once written (*Queer Books*, 1928) that the only good thing about Prohibition was that it shut this genre down, but for over a century, stories by and for women about long-suffering wives whose husbands drank their families into the poorhouse—and the grave—flourished. How many hundreds of tracts, pamphlets, *Blue Ribbon Army* magazines, and the occasional dime novel had V.K. pored over? Pour me another one, microfiche machine!

Thus V.K. Kunti's scholarship, his work. But his poetry was something different. His poetry was the idle pastime of his idle hours, his idle thoughts of an idle fellow. He had published in the school's literary journal, *Old Wreck Review*, one poem per semester for several years now, each a couplet with the name of a heroine from classic fiction travestied for our amusement.

<blockquote>
Daisy Miller:
Rome will kill her.
</blockquote>

Or:

<blockquote>
Lily Bart
Quashed a fart.
</blockquote>

Yes, yes, the audience should say upon reading this demicleri-hew, *that is exactly what Lily Bart would do.*

Clearly V.K. did not want to reveal which poem he would be reading on Saturday, perhaps for the sober reason that stating the subject would be reciting half the poem. Oscar noted with some degree of smugness that the attempted distraction—the joke—had failed only because this schmuck with his smart vest and his designer glasses had lacked a rudimentary knowledge of paleontology.

"No, I mean—you know how an apatosaurus gets called a...". But V.K. never explained. He never made it clear. This guy, this guy would just have to come to the reading to learn what was going on there.

Oscar picked up for $0.49 *The Crayon Papers* (1883; a posthumous miscellany) by Washington Irving, and they walked home. While Oscar hung up his hat, V.K. went to the bathroom, started his nervous dance with the door—which then snapped into place, all of a sudden. V.K. did not cry out *eureka!* or even *aha!* but the sigh of understanding he made just then...Oscar stood there in the hall by their bedroom, staring stupefied at the bathroom door, ~93% closed.

· 18 · This was the day · Albiorix, examined and planned around · King of the World · A shadowy figure · Paul Bunyan, his simulacrum · The boys go out drinking · The legend of Little Marty · Back-alley brothel · A missed opportunity ·

This was the day.

Now some things are easy to find while you sequester yourself in your apartment and make plans. The time of Johnson's presentation was easy to find, because it was in the dossier. We set it here, for reference, in military time: 19:00.

The times the *technology...conference* was open were easy to find, because they were on the website: Friday: 15:00–20:00. Saturday: 11:00–17:00.———For convenience, perhaps we should also reiterate: V.K.'s poetry reading: Saturday, 18:00; "charity" ball: Sunday, 19:30. The hits keep coming.

What technology people were to confer about was also easy to find. Announcements of some "exciting new" websites; robotic arms for amputees; computer-assisted eye surgery. Typical nerd stuff, no good for anyone. But Johnson's presentation, where he would unveil some code blah blah autonomous car blah blah—this was presentation that got the blink text. This (a few quick searches confirmed) was the thing about which everyone was talking.

(Also on the Albiorix website: Albiorix was named for a proposed but not yet confirmed moon of Saturn. In case you were wondering. "The compound should mean king or ruler of Albio, a word which may be identified with the Welsh word 'elfyth,' used by Welsh poets in the sense of the world or the universe: so we may suppose that *Albiorix* signified king of the world" read text that had clearly been taken without critical review from some public domain book. In case you etc.)

Less easy to find was how (at this late date) to acquire passes to said conference. There were separate applications for press, for industry, for thrill-seekers, each one quite lengthy and inconvenient. Did this address field have a drop down menu for each letter? Long before he had even reached the payment screen, Oscar decided to abandon this world of forms, turn off the computer, and make his plans.

For Oscar was on a mission, and the mission was to avoid killing an idiot kid who might be smarter than he'd assumed.

Everything depended on getting to the conference before Johnson, so Oscar headed into Manhattan early. He had been acquiring items he could not afford to leave unattended, and therefore his messenger bag held not only a wrapped-up gun but also Monica Dixon's invite; also a flashlight, a paperback copy of *The Collected Poetry of A.P. Herbert* (1948) to read on the

111

subway, and, just in case, a clipboard. Upon disembarking, he first stopped and looked in at the offices of Eradication Age over on 55th Street. Under the curtain he could see that the sacks of mail were gone, just a sweet disorder in the dust showing where they once had been. After that it was a quick twenty-minute walk down Tenth Avenue to Albiorix. People were already queued up on the sidewalk.

Oscar had had no doubt that even passless he could bluff his way into the conference with a clipboard and bluster, but he decided it would be easier to keep the subject outside the venue altogether. Also, based on how many irritating signs and advertisements for Albiorix that the Sheraton sported on its outside, the inside must be a hellscape. "I'm not getting in there" etc. So Oscar walked the queue, making sure M. Johnson wasn't in it already. Everyone was talking about the car thing. It would be the Segway of 2003. It would change the world. Oscar stopped to quiz a few people about it, and every single one of them seemed most excited because they thought they'd be able to hack into the self-driving cars and force people to have autoduels. But this was probably selection bias, and Oscar by instinct always sidled up to the worst humans with the craziest eyes.

The doors opened and the badgeholders streamed in, and Oscar paced the sidewalk for another half hour before Mordecai Johnson and Michael Wang hove into view, presumably on the crosstown walk from Grand Central. Oscar advanced to intercept them well before the hotel entrance. Everyone was glad to see everyone.

And at the intercept, Oscar watched as a tall, shadowy figure slithered by. He had clearly been following the pair. He had on false mustachios. He gave Oscar a meaningful look and a nod, too, as he passed. Oscar's head turned to follow the figure's progress down the street and away, but he never once let go his grip on the boys' arms, he never once stopped talking.

"I had to come to see your big announcement," Oscar explained, in case there was any suspicion in the air. "You nervous?"

"Of course," said Mordecai, who looked terrified and even shorter than usual. Oscar was also terrified, but it made him the tallest he'd ever been. He looked like a lumberjack. He looked like an outlaw biker. He looked like a man among pygmy ballerina toddlers. This was Oscar's secret, and when he cast his eyes back and forth, scanning for more shadowy figures, it just looked like he was surveying his kingdom. "King of the World." He said:

"We've got to get you a drink, calm you down." And: "Come with me."

"I can't go anywhere, I've got to present," Johnson whined. To Oscar, saying one was going *to present* sounded like something a baboon in heat did, and he could not help grimacing. But even his grimace looked like contempt. He would not be distracted from his plan.

"That's not till seven, right? We'll be back in plenty of time. There's so much we can do in four and a half hours."

"I wanted to see the robotic arm," said Michael Wang.

But Oscar had placed around their shoulders his arms, mere flesh and blood though they were. He steered them first to a nearby bar and grill and hid the kids in a corner while he bought shots. He carried these over and if one turned out to be an empty glass he'd swiped off a table and secretly filled with water from a flower vase—well, the other two glasses were full of gin.

"I get so nervous," Johnson said. "I know I get so nervous."

113

"It's all in your head, kid. Another drink will fix it."

"I want to throw up, but I know it's just psychosomatic."

Michael interjected, "My sister thought she had a hysterical pregnancy once, but it turned out she didn't." Oscar turned and looked at him. "It was pretty awkward," said Michael.

"You need to drink, too," Oscar said. And, indeed, after a couple of shots Mordecai and Michael were loosened up and stupider and willing to go to a "better" bar that Oscar knew, just a subway ride away.

"I really do have to be back by seven," Johnson warned.

"Just keep track of how long it takes us to get out there," Oscar suggested. "They you'll know how long it will take to get back. And if we run late, we'll just hop in a taxi, get back lickety-split." He hustled them onto a train to Brooklyn and kept them keyed up and not thinking by telling the story of the time he was in an illegal basement casino helping an old roommate cheat at five-card draw by standing behind the dealer and peeking at the top cards as he shuffled, but then the house detective "made" Oscar, and was watching him so closely that Oscar couldn't signal; Oscar wanted to tell his roommate to drop the deuce and go for the flush, but he couldn't signal; so he shat himself, and they won four thousand dollars.

"Why?" asked Michael. "Did you flush afterwards?"

"No, no," said Oscar. "There was no toilet to flush. I—oh, I'll explain when you're older."

"We're going to see something wild," Johnson stage-whispered to his coeval.

But this was Oscar's problem. 4 PM was not the wild hour. He rode as deep into Williamsburg, Brooklyn, as he thought he could get away with, and hustled the boys into another bar, but they were clearly getting antsy. These were just bars. Old

Polish men quietly sipping old Polish *wódka*. The logical thing to do was have a quick drink and go back to Albiorix, and this was just what Oscar was trying to prevent.

"To be fair," explained Michael, "this is a little lame."

"What are you talking about? This place is famous. The patrons are the absolute dregs of humanity. See that guy over there? That's Martin Bullock, the kiddie porn king of Brooklyn. You know how he does it? His crackhead parents, when he was a toddler, started farming him out and made a bunch of sick pornos. The guy appeared in thousands of hours of video before he was thirteen. He's like the world's most famous child porn star. Little Marty Bullock, you've heard of him, right?"

"I think I've heard of him," said Johnson.

Little Marty's parents (the fiction continued) got arrested and locked away and immediately prison-murdered, so Martin bounced around the child care system, eventually coming into possession at age eighteen of the only assets his dumbass parents had owned, viz. thousands of hours of pornographic video featuring none other than Martin Bullock. These would have been seized as evidence of course, except that Martin owned his own likeness. He needed access to the videos, which were the primary evidence of his own decade of victimization. And since he had both a legal and a moral right to the videos, no one could stop him from taking them away, from making copies and from selling them. How can you arrest a man for selling pictures of himself? Martin became the world's only child pornographer whose business was 100% legal. There were wrinkles, though: Comstock laws kept him from distributing his goods though the postal service, and internal standards and policies kept other, cautious carriers from moving them across state lines, so he almost exclusively did business in New York.

Also, it was incredibly illegal for anyone *except* Martin Bullock to own the wares he was copying and selling, so cops tended to hover around him, waiting to arrest anyone else who purchased the video chronicles of little Marty Bullock...

One by one, every sad-sack day-drinker got assigned to him a similar story of scandal and intrigue. But the restlessness of Oscar's audience was evident. He was losing them. They were even drinking slower.

"Okay," said Oscar at last, standing up. "What do you guys want to do?"

Go back to Albiorix.

"I mean before that. We have plenty of time. Do you want to taste human flesh?"

They did not.

"You don't have to keep it down. Cannibulimia, so-called, is rather tony these days."

They did not.

"How about a nice art gallery?"

What in the what now?

"Ha ha! I was just testing you. Do you want to get laid?"

That one. They wanted to get laid.

"Can't we get laid tonight," asked Michael, "as a celebration?"

"Tonight?" Oscar laughed. "Did you already schedule it? Do you think on a Friday night, of all times, you can just waltz right in without an appointment and say, 'I want to get laid right now'? We've got to do this now or wait for Monday!"

"But my parents will be back before Monday," Michael protested.

"Exactly! Let's go now, get you a quickie."

Johnson looked a little hesitant. "Are we...paying for it?"

"Of course not," said Oscar. "I'll just cash in a few favors."

And in the end that idea was too alluring to avoid. They took another train, further into Williamsburg. "We've got to make this quick," Johnson said, sneaking peeks at his phone and the time.

"We'll just cab it back," Oscar said. "You don't want your virginity to show when you're up on stage, do you?" He could almost feel bad about what he was doing—he had honestly never poured forth such an effluvium of peer pressure on anyone.

"I really envy you," Mordecai Johnson said tipsily. He explained that as a gay man, Oscar could afford to have a level of contempt for women that Johnson himself would never be able to achieve.

Could *almost* feel bad. But all he said, was: "Slow down. The one thing you don't want to look is eager. Don't jog; don't even walk; you've got to *saunter*." This had the advantage of looking like good advice while at the same time ensuring that their saunter from the subway to the ostensible brothel took longer than it should have.

"Is this a snuff brothel?" asked Michael Wang.

"Of course not! Snuff brothels are booked weeks in advance, even for early afternoon sessions."

"It's not really early afternoon any more." Johnson was glancing at his phone again. "How much further?"

"Not far now, Smurfs." This was the delicate calculus—not literally calculus, of course, don't worry about that—of how far away from the Sheraton he could push them, and they were reaching their Beas River, where the Macedonians mutinied against Alexander; their terminus, in other words. So Oscar halted his troops in front of a narrow suitably-looking gap between two buildings. "Here we are. Wait here while I arrange everything."

In front of him the alley twisted and snaked like a setting from a Daredevil comic. On the walls were not the comforting graffiti we all know and love (*COPE*; *Andre the Giant has a posse*) but strange new innovations (*Abramowitz is a neo-classicist*; *free Jomo Kenyatta for real this time*) to confound and confuse. Oscar squeezed his bag for the reassuring heft of a gun he couldn't remember if he'd loaded or not. Then he headed down a ways and hid behind a bubbling trash can for as long as he thought he could get away with. The murmuring of the troops was getting worse as he reappeared.

"Okay, so I don't care who goes first, but it's one at a time," said Oscar, "and remember we're in a hurry, so don't take too long. Two words of advice. Make sure the guy wears a condom, no matter how safe he says he is. And it's normal to bleed from your anus a little the first time, don't worry about that. So who's first?"

The two lads stood there dumbfounded. Oscar let the long moment lengthen.

Finally: "Wait. Who's going to wear a condom?"

"The top," said Oscar.

"Is that us?"

"Oh. I can try to arrange that, if you'd prefer."

"Is this brothel...what kind of brothel is it?"

"We have already established that it is not a snuff brothel, and I don't know a generic term for the other kind."

"No, we mean..." Mordecai and Michael looked at each other. "We mean..."

And Oscar kept this Abbot & Costello routine dragging on. He quibbled on every term. He misunderstood every statement. Finally he said, "Ooooooooh!" and even this, the O of realization, he milked for duration. "You wanted to have sex with a *female* prostitute. I'm sorry, I totally misunderstood."

But now it was late. Now it was time to speed back to Albiorix. As promised, they got in a cab.

And this is the thing about New York City. The subway is slow. At certain times of night, it is very slow, and at four in the morning, Oscar could have driven from his apartment to Yale, say, some seventy-five miles away, in less time that it would take him to ride the subway to N— Y— University (~six miles).

But at four in the morning there is no traffic. When there is traffic, things are very different. At 6:30 on a Friday, driving from Brooklyn to Midtown Manhattan is a fool's game, played by many, many fools.

When Johnson's presentation started (or should have started) their taxi was still on the Williamsburg Bridge. When it ended (or should have ended), their taxi was still trying to turn off FDR Drive.

"This is the worst traffic I've ever seen," Oscar lied, and the sullen cabbie was not about to contradict him. Johnson removed a thumb drive from his pocket and stroked it wistfully. Oscar wondered whether he should grab and swallow it, but decided there had to be a backup somewhere. "Look," he said. "Look, you missed your presentation. That sucks, and it's on me. I'll make some calls, pull some strings. You know I know people. You can do your presentation tomorrow, and that leaves us all night. Tonight we're going to party."

"Are we going to get laid?" asked Johnson.

Oscar wavered between "That ship has sailed" and "Guaranteed," and he went with "Guaranteed."

Michael said, "If we miss the nine o'clock train, there isn't

119

another train until midnight."

"Oh, you'll miss the nine o'clock train," Oscar said. "Guaranteed," he said.

· 19 · Car talk · The Coxman appeareth · A summary of events · The burnout joins, but only for a moment · Never worry about train schedules · Two disappearances · Cocaine is frankly not a very 2003 drug, but some people are retro · A legit fight ·

They took the cab all the way to Queens (because it would have been too obvious for Oscar to say: Let's take the train, it's quicker) and it was a long ride and Michael Wang talked so much about cars that Oscar feared that the two of them might be a collaborative duo, the J&W Autonomous Car Co., and he would get instructions to kill them both sooner or later. But actually, Michael just liked cars. He was boring, so Oscar kept cutting him off to tell stories of his own sexual prowesses and triumphs.

Once in Astoria, Oscar brought them to a bar he kept his hand in, nights when V.K. was burning the ol' midnight oil. He kicked down the door and shouted something about swinging dicks, and someone yelled "It's the Coxman!" and Michael giggled with delight.

"Have a few more and we'll look for some gash to get you buried in," Oscar said, and then he beat his chest kreegah Tarzan-style. He had picked a good place where even this early they tolerated his performance art.

Oscar's first suggestion to the boys was that they should hang around outside a tattoo parlor and wait till someone underage came by asking for a labial piercing. When she was turned away, one of them could step forward, claiming to be an experienced piecerian and offer to do it for free. "I used to get so much play with this method." Michael, though, prudently pointed out that they had no place to take the girl to pierce her, nor any even facsimile piercing needles, and furthermore the odds of this one particular set of circumstances happening not once but twice tonight (one for him, once for Johnson) was vanishingly slim. This last objection was in fact the very reason Oscar had proposed the plan, but he permitted himself to be talked out of it. His next proposal was *one more round!*

And then—but do we need to do this? Do we need to itemize every filthy story and every unwatered whiskey? When Victor Hugo wants to skip a scene, he says, "there are things which we must not attempt to paint; the sun is of the number." When Harriet Beecher Stowe is too lazy to describe something, she claims that "the immortal description of Washington Irving has saved us the trouble of representing in detail" that very thing. Is not the gradual degradation of two already-degraded sophomoric almost-juniors like enough unto the sun? Did not Rip Van Winkle ("naturally a thirsty soul") imbibe and overshoot his next appointment? Aren't we all on the same page here?

Perhaps a summary of the degradation will do. So: "First the Five Star, then the People's Bar": They crawled—at first not literally—from pub to pub, and Oscar wove mighty tales of the denizens therein. Most of these tales were false, but there were enough actually crazy people in any given bar that some of the accounts of knifings and gunrunning had an aura of plausibility. They got thrown out of one place for excessive rowdiness, which was quite a coup, and denied ("you've had enough") service in several. There were many requests to go to a strip club , which of course Oscar would not have been able to locate had he wanted to, and "see some boobs"; so finally Oscar explained that such requests were homophobic and they stopped. The night started out gray and oozed towards rainy. It was no fun, but Oscar pretended he was having fun, and in this way he was no different from everyone else.

Somewhere along the way they picked up an old drinking acquaintance of Oscar's, an itinerant acid casualty named Keith Cazzo, who quickly and ineradicably fell under the impression that these two young charges were Amish kids on rumspringa. Keith was handy because he would hallucinate terrible stories about Oscar and relate them in graphic detail, giving our hero a chance to catch his breath, thereby keeping up a constant stream on nonsense, which was important because if Johnson had a chance to think he'd realize he was miserable, and if Michael had a chance to talk he'd talk about cars. Everything was louder and livelier at this time of night, and from the open doors of some venues Boom Bands were playing, but Oscar selected only the grimmest and least desirable bars, to prevent a frisky bouncer from frisking the pistol out of his bag. There was some calibration going on. If Oscar pushed the gang too hard, they'd end up in a neighborhood where people did needle drugs openly on the street, where the truly hopeless, toothless tricks skulked together in packs they pretended were gangs, and stripped outsiders clean like piranha. Oscar tried to keep things just this side of the piranha. They missed the nine o'clock train.

"There's no train after midnight, so we really need to catch that one unless we both find girlfriends to sleep over with before tomorrow," Michael said.

"I'll drive you, don't worry," Oscar said. "Where do you live, anyway?"

Michael answered.

"I don't care if it's appalling, just tell me where—"

But no, no, a misunderstanding. The answer was Pawling, N.Y. The Metro North rail they had to take was two hours with a transfer this time of night, so driving would be quicker anyway.

"...then he managed to slip out of prison by hiding *inside* a fat man's corpse..."

"Oh, Keith, you flatter me," said Oscar to the old hippie. They were sitting in yet another dive bar, although at least this one had makeshift tables made from giant wooden industrial spools. The glasses were lined up and spilled a little and drunk and turned over and called "dead soldiers" and knocked off and shattered, again and again.

"Are you too drunk to drive?" Michael asked. Michael was too drunk to drive. He was so red that Keith Cazzo immediately began assuming he had spent the last two weeks on a raft at sea.

"Don't be an idiot, Fluffer," Johnson said. "You're just underestimating Oscar's stanima. His stamina. Stanima." Johnson stopped, puzzled by which one was right.

"Oh, I can help," Keith said, pausing in his second-hand losengerie to contribute something stupid. "Just use this mnemonic. Animals emanate minimal cinnamon..."

"Aminals..." said Johnson.

"And inimical, abdominal M&M enemas..."

"Aren't all emenas abdonimal by definition?" He was pooing very doorly, Johnson was.

"...contaminate intimate ham and eggs..."

This went on for a long time. Finally Oscar realized Michael was gone. He grabbed his messenger bag and got up to look for him and discovered he'd wandered into the men's room to

123

puke and had fallen in with a "bad crowd." They were doing bumps of cocaine off the rim of a urinal, and they'd decided to let Michael try some in exchange for articles of clothing, starting with his pants.

Since by this time of night Michael's pants (Oscar induced) would soon be discarded anyway, he figured it was not much of a loss, and he did manage to negotiate that at least some of the contents of Michael's pockets—his house keys, for example— be returned. Oscar paused a moment with the keys to take his handcuffs off. So that was some old business you'd probably forgotten about wrapped up neatly.

As he led a pantsless Michael out of the bathroom, though, Oscar realized that the evening was growing out of his control. He realized this because a coked-up Michael Wang was talking *nonstop* and *really fast* about lots of things but especially all the terrible deeds the people in the bathroom could have done to poor Michael, but didn't. This sounds grim, but at the moment Michael's imagination was trapped in some junior high fugue, and catalog was all: wedgie, swirly, wet willie...

Oscar made it back to the table, where Keith was passed out, a pair of Groucho Marx glasses hanging half out of his pocket. "Where's Johnson?" Oscar asked the unconscious man. "Well," Oscar added, "I don't think he could have gotten very far in the state *he's* in." He left Michael asking the hippie's lolling head, which was leaking—tears, snot, drool—from most of its holes, if Indian burns were offensive or just painful, and poked around outside in the cramped little smoking patio. A mandatorily smoke-free bar was novel enough in 2003 that the smokers' eyes all burned with rage as Oscar opened the door. But Johnson was not there, so he shut it.

When he passed Michael Wang again, the boy was still on his

list of terror he'd escaped: noogie, pantsing, pinkbelly...

Keith woke up suddenly. "You mean Pinkberry," he said. Then he chuckled to himself. "Asians, am I right? They're crazy for it." He didn't actually say this, of course; there were no Pinkberries in New York, if anywhere, in 2003; but this is the kind of thing he would have said, if he had been able to regain consciousness and the times had been different. Certainly he was not perspicacious enough to ask Michael how, if he had escaped pantsing, he nevertheless lacked any pants.

Oscar wandered forever in circles until he found Johnson in a corner leaning forward and speaking to a woman. This had been the perfect camouflage for Johnson, and Oscar had walked right by him half a dozen times, not processing that such a scenario was possible. The woman in question—her hair, like everyone's, was of a nondescript color, and she was probably taller than Johnson, although he was too wobbly to make the comparison fair. One lazy eye of hers sleepwalked upward and away. She was possibly a college student, or at least she was wearing a Fordham T-shirt.

For a moment Oscar wavered. Clearly he had to do *something*. If Mordecai Johnson actually managed to negotiate leaving with a companion, Oscar would have no way of making sure he missed the Saturday tech conference, too. One head of this tête-à-tête must be removed, as Hercules perhaps said to the hydra. Oscar would have to find some way to make Johnson appear unappealing and unattractive.

Oh, but Johnson was several steps ahead of him there. As Oscar Cox was still wavering, he saw the woman slap Johnson and turn and head for the ladies' room. Johnson wobblily pursued her, shouting, "You think you're so much better tham ne?" It was easy for Oscar to step in his way.

125

"Come on, your Wang buddy's got himself coked up, and I have to drive you home while he's still aware enough to give directions."

"Lemme at her, I'm-a go get her," said Johnson.

"You'll just make a fool of yourself. Come on."

"You said it," Johnson cried. "You said the strongest thoughts and the fairest women. You said we take them!"

Placing the reference took a moment, and even then Oscar had no idea how to explain the many levels of irony the later chapters of *Thus Spake Zarathustra* were supposed to be nested in, nor was he certain he'd made any of that clear when he'd supplied the quote. So he fell back on bluster, grabbing Johnson and dragging him sideways. "We're not taking anythi—" he said; but then Johnson broke away and started a lurching approximation of a bolt for the powder room door.

"I'm gonna stick my dick in her eye socket," Johnson said, which, come to think or it, may also have been a reference to certain yarns Oscar had spun earlier. Unsure what else to do, Oscar punched Mordecai Johnson in the pan. He had never thrown a punch with sincerity before. The usual way of saying that is: a punch thrown "in anger," but Oscar wasn't angry, really, just terrified and confused.

"You cocksucking pussy," Johnson said and belted Oscar so that he fell on the floor and hit his head on a giant industrial spool. A pitcher of beer wobbled off its edge and landed, spout-down, on Oscar's chest.

"Party foul, bra," someone said, but Oscar heard it from a long way away. He felt as though he were hovering on the edge of sleep, as though his bed had crept into the bar and coiled its soft self around him while he wasn't looking. On the other hand, everything was wet and uncomfortable, and he had apparently turned into a sow with large piglets suckling at his teats. No, that wasn't right either. He opened his eyes and found two or three young men trying to suck the remnants of their PBR out of his shirt.

"I'll buy you a new one, get off," he slurred. But beyond them he saw, what was even worse: the Fordham woman pasting Mordecai Johnson in the face again and again until he fell bleeding to the floor.

"Did you kill him?" Oscar asked with mixed emotions as she whipped her head around and glared at him, thunder in her brow.

· 20 · The revenant · The vulture eye · An empty house · New distractions needed · Return of the flames · A game of bluffs · Swordfish ·

Mordecai Johnson was not dead, but he sure looked bad, which is to say even worse than usual. This was a bit of a blessing because when Oscar woke V.K. up at one in the morning to borrow his car, he had Johnson as a puffy, blood-spattered, rain-soaked, bedraggled visual aid to explain why he needed it.

V.K. washed Johnson's face off in the bathroom (door: wide open) while Oscar collected ice cubes in a dishtowel. They wrapped another towel, like a kilt, around Michael Wang's Y-fronts. Everyone had instant coffee. Then Oscar tucked V.K. back in—don't wait up—and the three roustabouts limped to the car. The whole way north, Johnson lay in the backseat moaning.

"How will I give a presentation looking like this?"

"We'll get you some face lacquer, patch you right up," Oscar

127

promised. "Some PanGloss–brand face lacquer. 'The best of all possible face lacquers.'" This was one of V.K.'s jokes, and Oscar had only said it for something to say, because any moment that he was not speaking, the void was filled by the voluble Michael Wang. Wang spoke of cars. He spoke of fights. He spoke of the sights they passed. He read if not every then almost every sign obey posted speed limits patronize New York eateries fines doubled out loud. He mentioned casually and then with increasing insistence that he could fix the thumping in the engine that tell-tale heart-style only he could hear.

"You, know you're supposed to metabolize that stuff eventually," Oscar hinted.

"I think it's the coffee I've never had coffee before was that caffeinated? remember that time Scrote got beaten up by a girl?"

They all remembered that time. And Oscar remembered *The Revenger's Tragedy* (1606), and the lament of the rapist, named, oddly, "Junior," when condemned to death for his crime:

> My fault was sweet sport, which the world approves.
> I die for that which every woman loves.

The endless parody, which was Oscar's life, of a world caught in that sensual music had grown so wearying again that Oscar could barely keep his eyes open and on the road. For what was Johnson so willing to violate the laws of God and man, for what straining and funny faces? Wasn't Johnson fooling himself about sex? Weren't we all fooling ourselves about sex? If sex was such a great product, why did it need so much advertisement? Every TV show was a commercial for sex, except the news, which was of course a commercial for abstinence. *Good wine*, after all, *needs no bush.*

So the grunting and the faces and then the pores sphincter open and sweat oozes out; perhaps mucus rubs against mucus; until some other sphincter opens, internally, and goo rockets like a sneeze. It would be comical if it was not also so cthuloid. What a silly world, that each of us is fastened to this dying animal, like a limp rat in Oscar's case—who knew what women were fastened to? While Johnson had been half-right—that only as a gay man could you really express disgust at women's bodies and remain a good person—Oscar feared that, if once he started, he would have no place to stop, irregardful of sex or gender. How can I persuade you (Oscar might have said, if he could speak to you) that also beautiful and sublime and worthy of Parnassus is a story without sex (by which he meant, and here he had confused everything, as he always had to his tragedy, without love)?

"My face is like dog meat," whined Johnson.

"Sweet sport," said Oscar.

"Exit 6 Cross River Katonah I could fix that thumping thump thump thump hear it?" said the tireless demon that had possessed Michael Wang.

"Wait, what did you say?"

"Thump thump thump," he adumbrated.

The wipers shouldered the rain away, time and again, mile after mile.

The Wangs' driveway was empty when Oscar pulled in: Michael had left his own car at the train station, and the elder Wangs, as he had earlier intimated, were away. Michael did jumping jacks on the front porch, asking, "Does coke have caffeine in it?" and how do you even answer a question like that?

Once in the house, Johnson slunk off to whatever guest bed he'd been using all this time. Oscar, stone cold sober, decided without asking to crash here. It was three in the morning now. He lay down on the couch and had no problem slipping off to sleep, even though Michael was puttering and clanging through his dreams.

"Thump thump thump."

Everyone slept late, and Michael, found curled under the kitchenette table, latest of all. It was well past noon, and Johnson and Oscar sat at the table, Johnson's feet on the ottoman of Michael's kilted hip, eating cold cereal dry, for there was no milk in the fridge. The tea kettle bubbled its way into a boil.

"I'm sorry I let you down, Oscar," Mordecai Johnson said.

"You didn't let me down. You just need to learn to play hard to get is all."

There was something about the way Johnson was talking, though. As though he was trying to mean more than one thing at once. "I need to get to the conference for real now. You made your calls?"

That seemed straightforward enough. Of course, Johnson *should have noticed* that Oscar had had approximately zero minutes to make any calls unless he made them after Johnson had retired for bed. But who notices anything any more? "You're all set, last hour of the show. The keystone time."

"Is that the keystone time?"

"Sure."

Under the table, Michael said that he was sorry, too, and where was his wallet?

Oscar figured he'd offer these sports a ride, and just keep driving. Stay on highways and no one could jump out, even if the passenger figured out that he was shanghaied. It was cruel, but it would save the boy's life, at least temporarily. Afterwards Johnson could return to A—t and live or die as he saw fit, and Oscar could report to the Union that he'd put him in a sack and thrown him in the river, and if Johnson ever surfaced again, well: sacks these days. Not what they once were.

They changed clothes, all except Oscar, who was miraculously the only one who had gone the whole night without vomiting on himself, so it was less imperative. Somewhat refreshed they blinked their way out into the sunny driveway, and there on V.K.'s car...

"I'm going to kill you," said Oscar. There were flames painted on the sides of the car, like a "Big Daddy" Roth hot rod.

"Oh yeah," said Michael. "I forgot I did that."

But actually no one killed and no one died, because the flames were just magnets Michael had bought from some Kustom Kar Katalog. You stuck them around your car's fenders and they mimicked a paint job and then you could take them off. The looked pretty good, but since they'd just get stolen on the mean streets of Queens, Oscar persuaded Michael to peel them off and keep them for his own future use. A good laugh all around.

The three headed down I-684. Johnson in the back, Michael was sitting in the front seat again, quieter this time.

"Quieter," said Michael, after a while.

"Yes, you are," said Oscar.

"Does the car seem quieter to you today?" Michael asked.

And then the flames were back, shooting, this time, out from under the hood.

"Oh yeah," said Michael. "I forgot I did that too."

How were we going to keep Mordecai Johnson from reaching Albiorix? For once things worked out for themselves, eh?

131

As they stood on the side of the road, watching the flames rise higher and higher and engulf the car, Oscar said, "Michael, I could kiss you."

"Did you say kill?"

"Yeah, kill." Oscar was smiling.

Oh, they tried. They tried to get a taxi into the city, but first the police had to come and everyone had to give their names and show IDs and Michael's ID was an old library card he'd found in his sock drawer, which was weird, and Michael had to explain why he'd tried to fix the car without using word like *drugs* and why he had no wallet without using phrases like *traded it for drugs*. "Caffeine," he said, several times. Then they had to wait with the police for the tow truck, and then the tow truck had to wait for the fire truck, and after everyone had left and they were free to go they tried to call a taxi but Oscar had no cell phone and Johnson had forgotten to plug his in and Michael had swapped his for cocaine. They walked along the side of the highway for a long wet time until they got to a town and then they went to a Metro North station and people checked their IDs and Michael had to make excuses again and *that* took a long time and for a terrifying moment Oscar thought they were going to search his bag, but they didn't, and they waited for a train and rode it south but the conference was well over by the time they hit Grand Central.

"That really sucks," said Oscar as they stood around the big clock in the Grand Central Terminal. "Well, got to go."

"Hang on," said Johnson.

"No, I really got to go. My boyfriend is doing a..."

And he stopped, because Johnson had lifted the front of his shirt, and there sticking out of his waistband was the butt of a gun. No, not *a*; *the*.

"Hang on," said Johnson. "You owe me."

Oscar looked around to see if anyone had seen other than Michael (whose eyes were popping out comically), but all around the station people had their noses buried in that pot-boiler. Oscar nodded. He knew the tricks and he made eye contact and kept it, unendurably long, but Johnson stared right back. Oscar said, "You went through my bag while I was sleeping?"

"I was just heading for the bathroom to ralph, and I saw it had fallen next to the couch and there was a pistol half hanging out of it. It seemed like a good idea to see what else was there. There were no dildos at all."

"A dangerous man might use that as a dildo."

"You lied about the dildos."

"I said I had a dildo in there a week ago!" It was hard not to yell, but of course, some things were better said in a harsh whisper. "I do clean my bag out after a while." He hoped no one would remember that he'd told them the car was stolen.

Michael looked back and forth between them, clearly confused but perhaps also worried that if they made a scene he'd be carded again. All around there was no sound but the turning of well-margined pages and the distant yip of bomb-sniffing dogs.

"Well, you didn't clean your mail out of it," said Johnson.

Oscar knew enough of things to take a sharp intake of breath through his nose. Meaningly he said, "So you have it." Monica Dixon's invite.

"I do. And if I'd gotten to Albiorix I would have handed it over to you, no questions asked. But now I'm going to this orgy."

"It's a gay orgy."

"Nice try, Monica."

133

"Monica is my drag queen name."

"You'd never have a drag queen name that wasn't an atrocious pun," Johnson countered. This was true, incidentally. Oscar's hypothetical drag queen name, never acted upon. was Sybil Vein, and she was a vampire.

"What if it's not even an orgy?"

"A 'charity ball'? What else could it be? This is an orgy, and you stole this invite from a woman named Monica, and I'm going to go and get super laid."

Oscar considered his position. It seemed insane to bring Johnson into the maw of the very beast that had tried to devour him. On the other hand, it might be the last place they'd look, cat's-ear style.

"I'll take you with me as my plus one on one condition," said Oscar.

"When is this happening?" Michael asked. "Because my folks are coming back tomorrow."

"It's a plus one, Michael. One. And it's tomorrow night anyway."

Johnson said, "You're not really in a position to make conditions."

But this was now a game of bluff, and no one out-bluffed Oscar Cox. "Oh, come on, you can't think you know everything about this orgy just because you have an address. You didn't even know it was a masked orgy, did you? We'll need a disguise for you."

"That's the condition?"

"No; that's just me telling you things you have to know. Also what you have to know is we'll need tuxedos. I've got to get moving now, and I don't have time, but there's got to be a Men's Wearhouse still open around here. Go rent two tuxes for us, off

134

the rack. You'll have to eyeball what'll fit me, but I'm currently 6'2", if that helps, and manly. Then get some fake beards and mustaches and, like, nose putty at a Halloween store—you can find them in the Village. You'll sleep in Pawling tonight, and come to my apartment tomorrow at five."

"Actually, you need to be out of the house before noon, in case my parents come back early."

Johnson considered it. "Okay, I'll rent the tuxes, and see you at five, but I'm keeping the invite."

"That's fine with me. Is the password on the invite?"

"Password?"

"See. You need me, Johnson."

Michael said, "Also, you have to help me clean up the house tonight."

Johnson kept the gun.

Inside the messenger bag was a monkey wrench that Johnson had slipped in, for ballast. Only later did Oscar realize that a more ruthless and cunning Johnson could have taken the gun and the invite and not told him anything.

But by that point Book II had ended.

3

Book III: The Major Orcana

A feast is made for laughter...
−Ecclesiastes 10:19a

• 21 • Ogpu • Fan-favorite Peters returns • Phonemics 101 • Short chapters, very appealing • V.K. recites • Your kids, also, will be so cute •

The first thing Oscar did was buy two bananas since he hadn't had anything to eat all day except a bowl of Cinnamon Crispies, and, in case he had to drink a beer while pretending to drink twelve, he needed some food in his belly. Then he hurried down into the subway; he was running late. He stood on the overcrowded 6 platform and tried not to look at the buzzing lights, or let more than seven people touch him at once. "Hey, monkey! Hey, monkey!" tough guys and addicts and children catcalled him. He had no idea what V.K. would be reciting tonight. The initial plan had been to unveil his new, dactylic "Pamela Andrews":

Pamela *Andrews*
Loves both rakes *and* roués.

But further research had revealed that *roués* (as, verily, the accent acutely suggested) had in fact two syllables. And it was the old drawing board V.K. was back to.

Oscar fretted a moment that he should have put more effort into badgering his fiance about which composition he had chosen, but of course he had been distracted. *Everything was so difficult*, he almost whined. He was halfway through the second banana, out of breath, and in yesterday's clothes when he entered the Ogpu Bar, a little after seven. Schwartz was loitering by the entrance, a thumb marking his place in a black hardcover he was holding. "You know, bananas are the most caloric fruit," he said.

"Did I miss him?" asked Oscar.

"No, no, not yet. Some female has been all around looking for you. The one from Barb's."

So Oscar went in deeper, looking for Susan Peters. The bar was dark but quiet, especially for a Saturday night. Most people were sitting, listening respectfully to a woman on a small stage monotone into a mike:

I arise, bedhead, and slip on tight
pants, tight T, roll myself a
cigarette, and imagine before I
light it, that it is my ex....

Oscar nodded to a few acquaintances, swiped an empty beer bottle from a table more or less on instinct, and pretended to sip from it. He passed the shelves of vintage board games you could play ironically if you were drunk enough. He passed the art wall, which currently hosted an exhibit of a dozen photographs by a man who had written "transgressive" on his penis with a sharpie and then photographed it in bad light. He passed the pinball machine, which, to make the challenge greater, had one set of legs longer than the other so it was in a state of perpetual near-TILT. And there was Peters, swaddled in the shadows of the darkest corner, half-concealed by a potted plant, extra-hidden behind heart-shaped Kubrick–Lolita sunglasses. As always, Oscar could not tell if she was trying to look cool in a way he was unfamiliar with or trying to look uncool, simply and successfully.

"Oscar! I was hoping you'd show up."

"Of course I'd show—"

"Holy butts! What happened to you?"

Oscar realized he had no idea what she meant, and made a mental note to look in a mirror while he waved away any serious problems. "It's been a weird couple of days," he said.

"Tell me about it," said Peters.

Just then a woman with a clipboard strolled over. "Excuse me," she said.

"No! No surveys. Go away."

"Should I put you as *pro* then?"

"What? I don't even know what you're asking about."

"It's a proposal to run the Indy 500 and the Indianapolis marathon at the same time on the same track," said the clipboard.

Peters said, "What? No, that's a terrible idea."

138

"I'll put you as *con* then."

"Yes, of course. Now please give us some privacy." And she did. So Peters said, "Oscar, honey, I have dug up so much, so much you wouldn't believe on what *They* have been doing."

"You know about *Them*? I mean, about *They*?"

"I have so much to tell you." And she launched right into it. "Do you know what a minimal pair is?"

"Small...testicles?"

"There are languages where the sounds duh and tuh sound the same to them," she (but we're paraphrasing) said. "Yet we know they're different sounds because in English we have the words *train* and *drain*, and they're different. Or you know how in Japanese, they get *l* and *r* confused? *L* and *r* sound the same to a Japanese speaker. *Burūma* is a Japanese transliteration of *bloomers*."

"It's weird that you had that example ready like that."

"But we have words like *light* and *right*, so we know they're different sounds."

"Like *pink belly* and *Pinkberry*." Or the equivalent.

"Those words are called *minimal pairs*."

Oscar said, "But aren't *l* and *r*, like, objectively different sounds?"

"Of course they are. But lots of sounds are objectively different. The *t* sound in *top* and the *t* sound in *stop* sound the same to us, but ask your boyfriend's parents and they'll say they're different. They are different, but in English it doesn't matter. There's no minimal pair where one word is like *toga* with a voiced *t* and one word is *toga* with an unvoiced *t*, so there's no confusion."

"Top. Stop. Top. Stop."

"See, you can't hear it. It's there, but English speakers can't

139

hear it. But for any difference of sound you can hear—*v* and *f*, so *vine* and *fine*, *m* and *n* so *moat* and *note*—there's always a minimal pair. "

Peters's explanation was actually a lot more detailed and complicated and therefore accurate, but this is a thriller, and there is a gun and there was a fistfight and there's only so much getting bogged down in linguistics the form will bear.

"So," Oscar said, "what does this have to do..."

"It's the *t h*," Peters said. "Everyone knows that *t* and *h* together make two different sounds. There's *thin* and there's *this*. There *bath* and there's *bathe*. One is voiced and one is unvoiced. But the weird thing there are actually very few minimal pairs."

"*Bath* and *bathe* don't count—"

"Because the vowel sound changes, right. In fact, there are only two minimal pairs in English for the two pronunciations of *t h*: *thigh* and *thy* and *ether* and *either*."

"Okay, so they're different sounds."

"But look at this long-term plan. And this is really long-term. *Thy* is not exactly a common, living word. A couple hundred years ago, we stopped saying *thou* and *thy* and it's all *you* and *your* and how long before this archaic nonsense is forgotten altogether? And *also* a couple hundred years ago, like in the eighteenth century, and they blame it on King George I, but who knows, people started saying *eye-ther* instead of *ee-ther*."

"Let's call the whole thing—"

Peters's pocket started buzzing. "I'm serious, Oscar. Serious as Dillinger. And I'm not getting that." Her cell, she meant. "What happens when *thy* is forgotten, and people start pronouncing *either* so it doesn't pair with *ether*?"

"I just don't understand why this matters."

Peters leaned even more forward even more conspiratorially. She practically had Oscar by the lapels, only his shirt was just a T-shirt. She looked him directly in the eyes, and although Oscar frequently looked people in the eyes—as a trick, always as a trick—it was rare that someone else would *start* it. Also, she was wearing sunglasses, so her pupils weren't even visible until they got really close, until her nose and Oscar's were almost touching. There in the low-murmuring almost-hush of the bar, with the sound system droning some loser's voice

We dated for a thousand years.
We married were for three.
My insecurities and fears
Have lorn my love from me,

but the snapping of ice cubes in people's drinks still crisply audible, Peters hissed in the faintest whisper: "How are we going to talk about *They* if *They* sounds the same as *they*? How will we even know if we're talking about them? What are you going to say, 'They are behind all this'? It makes you sound like a paranoid loon!" The phone was buzzing again, still ignored.

"But that's just English," Oscar objected. "What kind of sinister secret society limits itself to the Anglosphere?"

"Oscar, do you know how many languages have both pronunciations of *t h*? Albanian. Welsh. The five thousand speakers of Elfdalian, maybe. Are the Welsh going to save us, Oscar? It's only in English that we even can talk about *They*, and only, we now know, for a limited time."

"Okay, okay; but what do *They* do?"

"So much! And—all right, fine!" The phone had started buzzing again, and Peters could not resist checking. It was her

141

boss, and she answered, of course. "What? No! Listen, Lance, they were asking about the Indy 500!" Still shouting into the phone, she turned and hurried away, her fate to be revealed later.

That left Oscar alone behind the plant—which also turned out to be an art exhibit: each leaf had written on it in sharpie (a cardboard standee artist's statement explained) the name of a casualty from the 1904 sinking of the steamship *General Slocum* in the East River, New York's worst loss of life until 2001—so he turned back, moseying through the bar, nodding at acquaintances. V.K. was probably sitting up near the stage, possibly with or near his parents, but there was no way to get up there without muscling through a bunch of little tables, and there was always a poet and always a microphone.

Cacophonous honeythistle
Barricades barnyard apertures
Pig sheep pig sheep pig sheep pig pig
Sheep.

Schwartz, sitting in a stool, turning pages, grabbed Oscar's arm as he passed. "Have you read this book?" he whispered. Oscar realized it was the potboiler, only with the paper dustjacket taken off "It's really smart! Also, the chapters are so short."

There was an M.C., of course, of the ladies and germs school, and at last he escorted V.K. onto the stage. "Ladies and germs," he literally said, albeit perhaps ironically, "next up we have *untitled*, read by Vagindra K. Kunti."

"I would like to point out that is not in the least how my name is pronounced," said V.K. good-humoredly.

Just then Oscar caught a look in the bar mirror of himself and the enormous black-green shiner he'd grown since last night. It was so horrible looking that the fact that Schwartz had managed not to mention it was either a testimony to his tact or evidence that he's never once looked Oscar in the face. By the time the start of semi-recognition—is that discolored pan really mine?—had returned Oscar to the bar, V.K. had finished his two-line recital. What had his poem even been? Kate Nickleby/ Sick'll be? But Kate's not the sickly type. Jane Eyre? A lot could rhyme with Eyre!

Everyone, as they had to, was applauding, but Oscar gave a wild whoop as well. Only now did he feel it, that one eye was squinty, and the visual world therefore lopsided. Whoop for V.K.!

"It's like poetry," Schwartz said admiringly.

Was it over? It was not over. A thousand thousand slimy things had yet to shuffle onto stage, and it would take forever. The guy after V.K. had the pan of a scorpion crudely tattooed over his pan. He started:

> A little weed, a little booze.
> We all agreed to get tattoos.
> We never settled on a place,
> So only mine was on—

Oscar Cox thought of all the planning he had to do before tomorrow, and nevertheless he stood there and waited.

"*I* think it's fake," said Schwartz.

And after all the poetry, when the lights came on and people hugged V.K. and slapped him on the back and Oscar came in for a chaste kiss and V.K. said, "Dear God, what happened to you?" with a gasp. As if he, too, had a scorpion pan.

143

"I took a few punches last night pulling that kid out of the bar fight," Oscar explained.

And then more people came up and slapped V.K. on the back and said congratulations.

"'Best wishes,'" Schwartz corrected helpfully.

The 'rents came up, with really a large number of great aunts and grandparents and aged people of all sorts, and they all hugged V.K. and then frequently (based on age, really) hugged Oscar as well for good measure, and split. Oscar could imagine V.K. saying that he got his forebears to attend, which was pretty good because even Goldilocks only had three bears; but V.K. said nothing of the sort. Peters had still not returned, but Oscar mentioned she'd been there.

Simple logistics dictated that Oscar, V.K., and Schwartz take the BMT back to Astoria together. They began their long walk to the Astor Place stop, and Schwartz monologued the whole way about ancient secrets and covert societies and how all that was hidden was being revealed by bold forayers into the truth such as—and here he thumped the novel's byline. Eventually, though, he remembered that this was supposed to be V.K.'s big night, and he brought himself to ask about the reading.

"What you read," he said, "it was so short. Was that just an excerpt or what?"

V.K. was struggling to suppress a smile. "I assure you," he said, "that poem is like Dorothy's worm medication."

"Huh?"

"It's in toto."

Before Schwartz could admit he had no idea what anyone was talking about, he suddenly started and dashed across the street so he could tell an interracial couple how cute they were. He actually had to run almost two blocks to catch up to them, and

Oscar just wanted to get home and get to bed.

Oh, Oscar!...he was so tired and also weary and annoyed at Schwartz and everything and scared and also tired, and just then, standing on Second Avenue, he blurted out, "Your car caught fire on the highway and burned into slag," and the look on V.K.'s pan was so surprised that Oscar didn't even get to add, as he'd planned, "but I saved your CDs."

• 22 • **What has Oscar been up to ostensibly all the time that he's been up to the things he's been up to?** • **Peters's downfall** • **Thriller or farce** • **Esau's blessing** • **The godfearers** • **Hands on** •

On the one hand, Oscar was so clearly not to blame (if you left out the parts that made it clear he was to blame) that all V.K. could say about a car that burst into flames fifty miles from home was: "Thank God you're all right." On the other hand, how could Oscar conceal the fact that he was up to *something*? All that sitting there, plotting and planning.

"What are you thinking about?" V.K. might ask.

"Math," Oscar might answer dangerously.

He'd been out Saturday tutoring, that much was clear, because V.K. could recognize Mordecai Johnson's one-AM face, even under the acne and contusions, as the face from the dossier, the A—t tutee. A wild night on the town must have gotten out of hand, and Oscar was the hero, dragging the boy to safety at some personal risk and injury, driving him and his friend back to Pawling, where his hypothetical Union-boss pop must live. A car used to local driving couldn't handle another trip on the highway apparently. The engine *had* been thumping, after all (some sources said). It all hung together, on paper, but surely there was something up.

"Is everything all right?" V.K. might ask.

"Carry the three, that leaves...oh! Sorry, I was thinking and I didn't hear you," Oscar might answer disingenuously. "Yes, copacetic."

Sunday meant brunch at Barb's, but no one was there: no Peters, not even Schwartz who was probably either sleeping in from his tiring poetry-based "night on the town" or trying to puzzle his way through the fourth-grade reading-level two-page chapters of his book.

Oscar snagged a discarded *Daily News* from a neighboring table. The front page was about Albiorix, and had no mention of Johnson or his self-driving car; the big news from the conference was the touting of a new website called MySpace. Everyone was talking (it said) about MySpace. Susan Peters was on page three—"*Post* Reporter: 'Keep the Races Separate,'" read the terse headline.

"What's happening in *Apartment 3-G*?" V.K. asked. "What's Margo up to?" So Oscar passed him the *News* and went hunting until he found a smaller article from a discarded *Post* briefly confirming that Peters would no longer be working for the paper after a recent racist diatribe.

Because V.K. would be staying in today, Oscar could not continue with his passive-aggressive habit of slipping off for hijinks once the cat was away. Instead, he established ahead of time that he had to go to a Union fundraiser, and the kid with the jacked-up pan would be coming by with tuxedos. This was probably not even suspicious at all. The two inamorati made tea and sat on the balcony and read their books. V.K.: *The Fountain and the Bottle: Comprising Thrilling Examples of the*

Opposite Effects of Temperance and Intemperance (1850); Oscar: *The Card: A Story of Adventure in the Five Towns* by Arnold Bennett (1911).

Do you think it's going to rain?

No, it's not going to rain.

Mordecai Johnson showed up a little before five. His face looked terrible, although some of the bruising had gone down. His face just looked terrible. He toted a backpack, immediately deposited by the door, as well as two tuxedos complete with shirt and cummerbund and tie. You wouldn't know this, necessarily, but this is not how Oscar usually dressed; but he tried his on and got a compliment from the kind fiance. Standard stuff. Johnson tried his on and looked like a jerk. V.K. had made a couple of phone calls and he headed out for dinner with friends. That left Johnson and Oscar.

"How much does he know?" Johnson asked Oscar.

"Not very much," Oscar told Johnson. He eyed the jacked-up pan. Getting your ass handed to you—was it true that it could change a man, make him hard? But Johnson was such a nerdy spaz, Oscar couldn't believe he hadn't had his ass handed to him regularly in the not-too-distant past. The wedgie to pink belly continuum. Was Johnson just playing at being a tough guy? Were the icy looks and clipped sentences all fake?

First (over Johnson's tepid objections) Oscar stage-glued a wispy mustache on the boy, and smudged under his eyes with burnt cork the dark circles of a nineteenth-century onanist. The nose putty on Johnson's nose made him look like a clown, so instead Oscar used it to build up his ears. Now Johnson had giant ears.

"How come you're not getting into disguise?"

"I've gone to so many masked orgies in so many disguises

that going with my normal face is the last thing they'd suspect."
Nevertheless, Oscar used the last of the putty, spread thinnest,
as a kind of concealer over his yellowing mouse. Then (most
importantly) he made a couple of cups of tea in case there was
no tea at the venue, and Johnson eyed his suspiciously. Did he
worry it was spiked? Did he worry it was not spiked? Had he
ever had a non-alcoholic drink after, say, noon? So Oscar drank
both cups.

"You got some schmutz on your shirt," Johnson mother-
henned.

"What? Where?"

"It might be your tea. Just make sure it doesn't stain." The
whine and the worry crept back into Johnson's voice as they
doubtless inevitably would no matter how many times he was
stomped to the curb, no matter how many tough-guy vibes he
tried to throw off. "I had to leave a deposit for condition and
everything."

"I'll pay you back, don't worry," Oscar, who had spent all
his folding money on booze, cabs, and tow trucks, said. He
retreated into the bathroom to spray some stain remover on
the tiny brown dots.

At the critical moment, as he reached for the bottle, Johnson
from far away said—and did he time it this way? was this part
of a plan?—"Why is my picture on your kitchen table?"

Oscar grabbed a bottle and raced down the hall. Where had he
left that dossier? Wasn't it under a pillow or in an underwear
drawer—but whose? How suspicious did this look, anyway?

And he was in the kitchen. Johnson was there, by the kitchen
table, of course, looking up in surprise. There before him, as
you may have guessed—we always play fair, or usually— was a
vintage promotional photo of a tuxedoed Cary Grant in a pewter

148

keepsake frame.

"Huh?" said Johnson. Perhaps he was reacting to Oscar's wild look, because he lamely added, "I was just joking."

"Oh," Oscar, suddenly blasé. "For a moment I thought you were featured in one of my porno mags." He turned around and headed back to the bathroom, giving the microscopic stain a couple of spritzes as he went.

There on the bathroom sink, when he reached it, was a bottle of Stain Scream. "Scream away your stains," said a cartoon banshee on the label.

Not out loud Oscar said, "If that's the stain remover sitting on the sink, what am I now holding in my hand?" And when he looked at the hand with the Mildon't–brand mildew remover "with bleach and other active agents" he did not, out loud, scream.

"Perhaps it will all be okay," he thought, gazing in the mirror at a perfectly fine tuxedo. As as he watched, a white flower opened up, centered on his heart, and blooming across the black lapels, first one side, then both.

He kicked the door shut. The first imperative was secrecy and *Johnson must not know.*

But of course he would know. Everyone would know. There was no real way to conceal this. The white shirt was only slightly discolored, and could pass in bad light, but the dinner jacket was now part tie-dye. This is ridiculous! Are we reading a thriller or a farce? (*Answer*: a thriller.)

Oscar held (in case Johnson left the kitchen) a towel in front of him as he slipped out of the bath and into the bedroom to dig out a black magic marker. He colored in the jacket's whitened parts as best he could, and this did not work so well.

Now you may imagine, based on your television programs,

that any home of two gay men would have an assortment of fancy capes that would go with this formal attire. You wouldn't know this, necessarily, but that is not how O. & V. dressed. No capes.

Oscar strode out into the kitchen with a curtain, folded in half, draped over his shoulders.

"Is that a curtain?" Johnson asked.

"This is orgywear. Shall I get you one too?"

"You look ridiculous."

"I was only joking," lied Oscar. He dug a winter coat out of the closet, slipped it on and the curtain off, and quickly buttoned up. Wind = free. Because Oscar lived in New York, his coat was black, and could therefore pass for dressy.

"Are you tardy?" Johnson said. "It's summer."

Oscar considered trying to pretend he was concealing an Uzi, or a bomb-vest, but settled on "It's much colder by the water."

They entrained, so to speak, at Astoria Boulevard, and (in order to avoid the Lexington line) rode the BMT to Times Square to switch to the IRT downtown. It was early enough on a Sunday night that the station was sparsely populated. Oscar and Johnson sat on a bench on the 1/2/3 platform, one seat safely between them. The light above buzzed, and Oscar kept his eyes level, but Johnson, like a rookie, looked up, which made him sneeze.

"God bless you," cried a cheerful voice from across the tracks, on the far platform.

Johnson wiped his nose.

"Did you hear me?" the voice cried. "I said God bless you. Hello? It's considered polite to say thank you when someone says God bless you to you."

Johnson looked at the floor, red-faced.

"Hello? Hello, I'm talking to you! I'm talking to you, turdface! Hey! Do you hear me now, turdface? I'm going to come over there and slit your throat—"

And the train pulled up between them.

It deposited Oscar and his charge at Fulton Street. "I've never been to this particular orgy before," Oscar said, "but I'm told it's really weird. It might be a slow build. Play it cool."

"Super cool."

"You have the invite?"

Johnson just nodded.

"You have the gun?"

Johnson just shrugged and smiled.

A brisk walk through the Financial District. What was happening down here? What did the I-bankers and stock-jobbers of the Financial District have, anyway? Manners? Virtue? Freedom Tower?

No, none of those.

Not yet, at least.

Not yet, old man.

A brisk walk to the hotel. Next week: monster magazine and horror convention; this week: private party. There were people in formal wear milling about on the sidewalk, and Oscar almost tried to join a queue before realizing there was none.

Fortunately moon-faced Walter Pilkoç waved a cane and advanced with a handshake (quality: hearty) and said, "Ah, the young seeker after knowledge! I was hoping I'd run into you!"

"When do the doors open?" asked Johnson, trying to conceal his erection.

"They're open, they're open. Walk this way."

And yes, he had a cane and a limp and an old-man shuffle,

but you can't, when the time comes you just can't. Oscar and Johnson moseyed after him, through a revolving door. Johnson had pulled the invite from somewhere, and a Prussian doorman/admiral took it and scanned it with some kind of light pen, and filed it away, and they were in.

"So those guys were just...waiting?" Oscar asked.

"On the sidewalk?" Walter said. "In a manner of speaking, yes. They are waiting for an invite. This way to the elevator. They are, as we say, godfearers."

"Godfearers?" If they didn't ask it, they might as well have. The question hovered there in the elevator.

"In the Roman Empire," said Walter, who apparently loved to tell stories of the ancient world, "Judaism was fairly trendy at times." The doors dinged and opened, and everyone stepped out. Walter led them down a fancy corridor with many ferns in many vases, but he walked very slowly, and he led them very slowly, and as he walked he spoke. "The trendy—they were Jewish converts, but they weren't full Jews. They weren't descended from Jacob, of course. They had no horns. But they also didn't get circumcised. They lived by the Law, but they also lived outside of it. They were demijews, called godfearers, hanging around outside the Temple but never allowed inside."

Oscar perhaps unkindly thought of Susan Peters, and her desire to exist in proximity to a relationship between two gay men. He most definitely did not think about himself. He said, "So these guys, they're hanging around outside because they're not ready to fully commit?"

"No, they're just too poor to afford a ticket."

"I'm already circumcised," Johnson said, sounding worried. "So, like, hands off."

This was the wrong attitude to have for an orgy, of course, but

Walter's chuckle indicated that it was also the wrong attitude to have at a charity ball. "No, no, my boy," he said, as he pushed open the double doors at the end of the corridor. "Hands on."

· 23 · The first circle · The mad parade · Amateur herpetology · Al Gore, revealed (a.k.a. ibid.) · Satyrs and Satanists · "I heard the Hall of Presidents at Disney World is so realistic, the animatronics turn into lizards at night" · The sharp sword with two edges · Fate of the world · The Mason Word, perhaps · The wonderful toilet · The wonderful fortune ·

It turned out there was quite a lot of multi-level marketing at this party. There was also an open bar, which kept Johnson occupied while he waited for people to take their clothes off.

It was not the best crowd for an orgy. It was a rather elderly crowd. Some of them wanted to sell you AmWay and some of them wanted to sell you Consolidated Products, but mostly they wanted to sell you themselves. The first-time poets with their chapbooks and the time-sharers with their time-shares were no match for the woman who knew the truth about fluoride or the anti-rock'n'roll man who had counted every appearance of the words "drum," "distortion," and "groupie" in the King James Bible (final count: 0). A European alchemist with a limp, gloved handshake who knew how to purify the soul as well as how to weave gold from the ether successfully bridged the two genera of sellers; he was looking for seed money that would blossom into 1. enlightenment and 2. gold a thousandfold. Of course he was.

Walter had already wandered away, and Johnson was long gone, so Oscar went around rattling the ice cubes in an empty glass he'd picked off the floor, standing in one circle and then another. He tried to look mysterious and later he tried to look interesting. It was not hard to talk to people, because everybody wanted to talk. "Are you going to take your coat off?" was one thing they kept asking Oscar until it became too obvious that he was not.

"Ah, this is the place," said an old woman wearing a brooch the size of her head, festooned with pointy bangles. "It's so rare in life that you get to see a true cross-section of society, all sorts of people united by only the common bond of seeking wisdom."

"But aren't you all filthy rich?" asked Oscar. "I mean we. Aren't we all filthy rich?"

And they were. And we were. And what were we seeking, if not wisdom? Enlightenment? The Mason Word, so-called? Ah, but we were seeking attention, and some of us were seeking the attention of *They*.

This was a ball, so the room was a ballroom, which is just another word for a room without installed tables or seats. What tables there were had been moved to the sides of the room, where they supported some finger foods and bowls of fruit. Behind a bar on wheels stood the only black person there, clad in hotel uniform (mauve vest); in front of the bar on wheels was a queue. There were deep red curtains around the perimeter, broken only for the double door entrance or to allow clear access to the fire exit ("alarm will sound"); and sometimes people slipped through the curtains, to secret recesses, and back again. Mostly, though, people just stood around, drinks in hand, and mingled. Some had nametags on.

"The young fellow you came with," a man tagged as John Boehner asked Oscar, "is he...well, he is a little reptilian around

154

the face, isn't he?"

"He's just ugly," said Oscar. "Like everyone else."

"And who but a lizard would wear false whiskers?"

A velvet-gowned, giant-headed woman named Marissa Hardon interposed. "Pah! I personally don't believe there are as many lizard people as everyone says." Her age was impossible to determine, but her armpit looked like the inside of a cat's ear. "Probably just one, just Al Gore."

"I'd like to go talk to him."

"Who? Al Gore," asked Oscar hopefully.

"No," said John. "Your cold-blooded friend."

"Don't!" said Oscar. But he couldn't help listening in terror and awe as Marissa Hardon nodded her oversized head and offered the following elegant proof.

1. The 1983 television miniseries *V*, despite its popularity and the prevalence of action figures in 1983, only spawned one toy for the American market: an oversized lizardman figure in the obsolescent 12" format usually referred to as a "doll."

2. Gore Vidal, when he traveled back in time from the future, took the absurd name *Gore Vidal*.

2a. In case it was unclear that Gore Vidal had traveled through time, why would he keep writing novels about time travelers if he hadn't?

3. Gore Vidal has often claimed to be Al Gore's cousin, the same way that mammals and reptiles are cousins.

4. If we look at Gore Vidal's absurd name, we can see that it reveals, homonymically: Gore: V-doll. Gore = V-doll. Gore is a V-doll.

Ergo: A lizardman. *Q.E.D.*

"Wait," said Oscar. "Honomynically?" But he shook it off. There was too much going on to get bogged down in ham and eggs now. Marissa's giant head eclipsed the light fixtures, and plunged Oscar into shadows. Later, Walter came by and explained that there was a new form of plastic surgery, where instead of tightening the skin doctors increased the size of the skull.

"She's like a Russian doll with a Chinese box," he added, and how does one respond to *that?*

And then: "This is the worst orgy ever," Johnson hissed at Oscar's shoulder. The lad was a little drunk. "We should have gone to the snuff brothel."

"Did you want to go to a snuff brothel?" a passing man with a walrus mustache and small pox scars asked.

"No!" said Oscar, steering Johnson away by the shoulders, as was his wont. He knew where this would end up. He knew how it would go. "No, he does not." And then he said to Johnson, but whispering: "Did you talk to an ugly, big-nosed fat man?"

"Yeah. He wanted to know where I was from and I said I was here for the tech conference."

"Don't tell anyone who you are! Don't even give clues!"

"Then I asked him when things would be starting to get interesting, and he said December 21, 2012, whatever that means. And then he asked me about prophylactics."

"Prophylactics?"

"He asked if I had a nictitating membrane. Do you think these guys have V.D.?"

"At an orgy? What do you think? Look, you'd better stay near me."

"You're not my mom."

"They might kill you. They might kill us."

"I'm not exactly worried: Everyone here is an ancient gay Jew. No offense."

BOOK III: THE MAJOR ORCANA

"I know that you mean it as more of a metaphor."

"Except the *old* part. That's super-literal."

"Excuse me, can I introduce the two of you to an exciting marketing opportunity?"

Excuse me. Excuse me, but what is it you want to know? Do you want to know why they all drank so wildly? "You can't be a satyrgahi without first being a satyr," explained Walter with a wicked wink—with the crook'd end of his cane he cocked a lampshade he'd set on his head—and Oscar was not in a position, he would not for some years yet be in a position, to know that one of those words was misspelled and mispronounced.

Excuse me, do you want to know why World War II was fought? It was over possession of the altar of Pergamos, "where Satan's seat is" (Rev. 2:13), explained one Herr Doktor Maximillian von Siemens, bad skin, bad hair. German archaeologists had brought this, the literal throne of Satan, to Berlin in 1930, and so the second-most-Satanic government on earth sat in Satan's seat. But Stalin (#1!) was envious, and coveted the altar; he goaded Hitler into invading Poland, knowing it would bring the West against him, allowing Stalin to lure the Germans deep into Russian territory so he could roll back through their strained ranks and seize Berlin, and therefore the throne of Satan, on which Vladimir Putin sits today. Did that clear up the turbid course of history for you? Because everyone here wanted to tell you something like that. And behind it all? *They* were behind it all. *They* had created a puzzle, which was generally called history, and many people here had a single piece of the puzzle, and sometimes the piece sounded irrefutable, but all the pieces were mutually exclusive.

The common element in each attendee, beyond, of course,

fabulous wealth and conspicuous consumption of alcohol (Johnson was back in the bar queue, incidentally), was a look of terror in the eyes. No degree of mad pleasantry could cover up the terror. "Some smiles look as if they had been done up in curl-papers over night," Carolyn Wells once wrote (1904).

There was terror that they were wasting thousands of dollars, but more than that they were terrified that they were wasting their lives. Either 1. there were no shadowy forces secretly weaving the tapestry of the world, unraveling our own efforts like Penelope at night, or 2. there were, but the same were coolly indifferent to these seekers of wisdom.

"Is there nothing *They* can't do? Really quite impressive," John B. said, and he looked around to see if anyone had noticed. But no whirlwind bore him to heaven. Perhaps a curtain rustled. Was that Keith Cazzo peeking out from behind it?

No. No, it was a mildew stain on the wall. An understandable error. "Hypothetically," Oscar asked, "if *They* wanted someone dead—not someone in this room, but someone hypothetical— why would they want it? What would they be after?"

"Well, the same thing they're usually after," said Walter, sidling up. The string of drinks had smoothed his limp into a sailor's rolling gait. "They seek the Mason Word."

"Right, right, of course. But what's the Mason Word?" asked Oscar.

General laughter. "Well, obviously, we don't know what the Mason Word is."

"Okay, sorry," said Oscar. "I meant: What *kind of thing* is the Mason Word?"

"Ohhhhh. Well." And the whole circle, four or five people not including Oscar, looked around awkwardly. "We're not really certain about that either."

"Some say the Rosicrucians know it. Some say the B.P.O.E."

"Some say that when you hear the Mason Word, reality peels away..."

"Ack!"

"No, no! It peels away like dryer lint. It is very satisfying."

"Whatever it is, it has to be important or *They* wouldn't be looking for it."

"Frankly, *They* could cut me open and eat me, and I'd be okay with it," said John B. "In fact, I'd welcome it!"

"The actions of *They* are more vital than ever," added a rather imperious British woman with a greenish seasick pallor that extended to her teeth. Walter had introduced her as the Countess of Peniston. "The fate not only of the world, not only of the universe, but indeed of the very concept of existence hangs in the balance."

Johnson was back and not very steady. "Listen, lady. If it were possible for the universe et al. to be eliminated that easily, it would have happened by now." He pronounced *et al.* "et all," like a hillbilly, and Oscar winced, assuming that someone here would have read, as Oscar had recently, that "no educated person pronounces a Latin abbreviation as anything other than the full words, e.g. *exempli gratia*." But Oscar had forgotten, somehow among the lizard-hunters and the Satan-hunters, that these people were all crazy, and if any clue was going to reveal them as outsiders, it would not be a misuse of Latinisms.

"Ah," said the Countess, her green teeth showing, "but it has."

"Sure, sure, lady. But I mean it hasn't happened recently." Johnson, as has perhaps already been made clear, was an unpleasant drunk, and suddenly Oscar realized that if they were caught it would not be because of any revealing slip-up and unknown secret grip, it would be because Johnson would vomit into a potted plant (which he, frankly, already had, while Oscar pretended not to notice) while abusing or assaulting people. Perhaps the only thing keeping the Countess from perceiving the belligerence of Johnson's tone was a misapprehension that when he said "lady" he meant it as a title.

Or perhaps nobility is trained to be polite to boorish commoners. The Countess laid a light green hand on Johnson's arm and said, "On the contrary, it probably happened about five minutes ago. It happens constantly! This universe itself, science shows, is less than fifteen minutes old. It just sprung into existence with all these false memories of events that never happened. We're only a few minutes of age; we just have brains that think they're much older."

Oscar laid his hand on Johnson's other arm, so he could pull him away quickly if necessary. "And so the universe will be destroyed..." he prompted.

"Probably in five or ten minutes or so, yes. And not just the universe, but the very concept of existence itself."

"Look," said Johnson. Both his arms were held, so he could not point in an accusatory fashion. "All we have to do is wait five or ten minutes, and if the universe is still here, you'll be proven wrong, okay.

"Oh, no, that's happened before. We've tried that experiment before. It won't mean I'm wrong, it'll just mean this conversation, and the last ten minutes, never happened. It was just part of the false memory of the world."

Johnson said, "But if the world is destroyed every fifteen minutes, how can the very concept of existence be threatened? The universe just pops up again anyway."

"No, no. Only *this* universe *existed*. There have been and there will be other universes, but they won't exist. They'll be something completely different: We wouldn't even recognize them. If we were still around to perceive them, that is."

"Imagine that," said John. "A completely noumenal world."

"No more," said Marissa, "lizards controlling our thoughts from a secret base in Tel Aviv."

"It would be marvelous!"

"Thrilling!"

"Phenomenal! No, wait..."

Johnson's pan, less poker-tempered than Oscar's, shared the question: *But how did she know? But how did any of them know?* So certain about everything, when there was no way anyone could have known any of it.

A shadow fell over Oscar. "The Mason Word," Marissa Hardon was whispering in his ear—"he who hears it, if he is in spiritual readiness, ascends. But if he is not prepared, the Word is wasted, and hearing it drives him mad." The moistly sibilant (*spiritual readiness ascends*) explanation distracted Oscar for a mere moment, but when he turned back he no longer held Johnson by the arm. In his hand, instead, was a monstrous and demonic face, which he realized, after a moment was a tiki tumbler. The paper umbrella was the clue.

John Boehner, meanwhile, had stepped into Oscar's place, as it were, and he had Mordecai Johnson's arm. He held it in a friendly, avuncular grip. Johnson's other arm, of course, was still held by greenish fingers. "Did you try the bathroom?" John B. asked. Asked Mordecai J.

"No, I just used that plant over there," said Mordecai J. with the honesty of the drunk.

"I mean at the tech conference you went to. I heard that hotel got these new miracle toilets."

161

Did Oscar think, *That's a weird thing to say?* But it seemed reasonably normal in comparison. And anyway, he was busy pretending to sip from the tiki head.

John B. was still waxing poetic on the toilets at the Sheraton: "They got Japanese models that wash your butt for you—"

"Japanese models!" Gravure dreams and sailor suits and that was enough for Mordecai Johnson.

"—and then blow it dry."

Johnson broke free, both arms, and bolted for the door.

"That's not what he means, you idiot," Oscar called after him, and: "You idiot, I'm your ride," which was no longer even true. But he, M.J., still had his con badge (or so Johnson explained to the ether) and nothing could bar him. From hotel reentry. Leaving behind only a Looney-Tunes cloud, he ran through the fire exit ("alarm will sound"); and no alarm sounded.

"They really are an excitable species," said John. Was it all an innocent mistake? J. Boehner and the countess walked off arm and arm.

"I have morgellons," Maximillian von Siemens nonsequitured, scratching himself. And this was before the epidemic, this was before anyone had heard of the disease. So he, too sounded crazy (also: He was).

Things did not end there of course. The hours dragged by, and the night limped on. "Crazy words, crazy tune." Oscar kept his ears open and his big mouth shut. He learned a lot, but all of it was wrong or false or absurd.

Gradually—and it did happen gradually—people began to realize that they were talking to each other, but only to each other. There was no one else here. There would be no recruitment.

"Not a single one of you is even a guru!" one fat man fumed, throwing his drink to the floor. He stormed out of the double doors.

"I'd frankly been looking for the Manson Word, anyway," a woman with a cadaverous face said. "Sorry about the misunderstanding." And she left, too.

"Is that it, then?" asked the Countess. "Is this really the end of the ball?"

"As René Magritte said at the construction site," Oscar added, glad for an excuse to leave, "this is not a drill."

Suddenly a mauve-vested figure appeared before him. It was the bucktoothed bartender, and he inexplicably pressed Oscar's hand.

"It's been a pleasure serving you, sir," he said, also inexplicably.

Oscar kept his hand cupped all the way out the doors and down the hall and down the elevator and out onto the street. The godfearers were gone. It was drizzling, and any trace they had even been there was washed away. In Oscar's hand there was a little piece of paper, no larger than a cookie's fortune. The date and time, the address on it, in the wilds of Brooklyn—all these things, or at last their ink, began to fade into oblivion as soon as Oscar laid his eyes on them.

• 24 • The origin of backgammon • The denouement • Freedom • First green •

Walter Pilkoç was up next to Oscar in a flash. His limp permitted only sudden bursts of speed, perhaps, because he took Oscar's arm and walked slower. They both walked slower. It was almost four in the morning and very wet, and no one was on the streets.

Some time passed in silence, and then: "I was thinking

about the question you brought up. A very good question! Do you know the story of Buzurjmihr?" Walter asked. Obviously no. "This was a long time ago, in the sixth century," Walter continued, "and not in Hatt-USA, as I call this country, but in ancient Persia. It happened that India sent the Persian Emperor a chess board and chess pieces, and bet him he couldn't deduce the rules from the pieces. But the Emperor's cunning vizier Buzurjmihr studied the pieces until he figured out the rules, and mastered the game, and defeated the Indian ambassador. Then he invented backgammon and sent the board and pieces to India, to see if they could deduce its rules in turn."

Seemingly at random they had ambled past the so-called "ground zero" and were now, the cooling wind in their tousling hair, down by the Hudson. Across the river Oscar could see the intermittent lights of the New Jerusalem. Like an obelisk over the riparian town towered the lambent clock of what Oscar had heard referred to as "Eerie Laocoön: A Plaza"—doubtless some sort of honomynical error.

Walter Pilkoç continued his pleasant tale on their pleasant stroll. "The point of this story, an old Persian one of course, is that no one could possibly deduce the rules of chess by examining the pieces. Similarly, no one can deduce the plans of *They* by studying their outward actions. Their games are too deep.

"But we are told Buzurjmihr did deduce the rules of chess. He could only have done this if he already knew how to play. Similarly, whatever it is that is happening, *They* already know all about it. We exist or resist at their pleasure. Do you understand?" He had stopped and was now facing Oscar. Between his huge jaw and his bulgy forehead, the actual features of his face were hopelessly receded into shadow. Also, when he spoke, jaw and forehead "approached one another like a pair of nut-crackers," which was horrible to behold.

He was now holding Oscar's wrist. His eyes, peeping from the shadows, were very close to Oscar's eyes. It was a little awkward.

"I'm very flattered," said Oscar, "but it was my friend, actually, who wanted the orgy, not m—"

But Walter was suddenly twisting Oscar's wrist now, bending it painfully so that his hand came open. With a demonic "Aha!" he plucked the little paper out. "I told you it was hands-on!" he crowed, as he zipped over towards a streetlight, limp gone. "I knew you looked a likely prospect!" He examined the scrap, first one side and then the other. "What?" He turned to Oscar. "What does this mean?"

Oscar could only shrug but also look terrified.

"Tell me what he said to you. Tell me what this means, or I'll kill you!"

"Why don't we all try to calm down?" Oscar said, but Walter with a click eased his cane in two, and attached to one half there was, smoothly unsheathing, a long wicked-looking blade.

"What a world dies with me!" Oscar said, and said involuntarily—you know, like thinking about math when someone brings up boobs. Then he elaborated in a saner fashion, "It's just a blank piece of paper. I know it's crazy, but everyone there was crazy, what do you want from me?" He prepared to turn and run and test his speed against the suddenly straight and limber legs of a newly spry Walter Pilkoç. But of course, the only place for him to run towards was a railing overlooking the Hudson.

Before the vain sprint could start, a voice rang out, "Deliver him!"

165

Two pans, Walter's and Oscar's, turned towards the voice, and it was the alchemist, his jacket draped over something in his right hand that pointed directly at Walter's cummerbund. Walter sheathed his sword, bowed first to the alchemist and then to Oscar, and hastened away and out of sight.

"Thank you," said Oscar.

"He bluffed," the alchemist said. His accent was possibly fake and possibly French. *Freedom*, rather, was what they called it in 2003, a strange time of freedom leave and freedom pox and freedom letters, when coffee came from a freedom press, and, after burning one's tongue on it, one might have to apologize with *pardon my freedom*. But the alchemist just said "And voilà!" He whipped off his coat revealing a hand holding nothing more exotic or dangerous than a glass alembic. "I also bluffed! Certain persons take things too much seriously. An alchemist, he sees his dreams broken every day. His experiences, no his *experiments* go up in smoke. His *plomb* remains *plomb*. He learns that all is ephemeral, and such knowledge softens the soul."

"That makes sense," Oscar said, as they strolled together to the subway. "Nothing gold can..." and here he glanced over his shoulder in case Schwartz was somewhere nearby and listening, "...endure," just in case.

· 25 · Peacock · Radio programming · Wink-wink Theater · A pleasant evening of music, excerpted · *Ipsos custodes?* ·

Thomas Peacock calls sex "that consummation which is most devoutly to be wished." He was being arch, but it's still a good quote. The point is that Oscar Cox had memorized the quote.

He'd memorized where it was from (*Nightmare Abbey*) and the date of publication (1820). There were times when Oscar Cox was good at memorizing things.

As a child he memorized all the amusing collective nouns for animals, starting with the ones that people actually use (pack of wolves, flock of sheep), through the ones that only exist so that anthologists can self-consciously include them in catalogs of collective nouns (murder of crows, crash of rhinoceroses) to the ones he made up (embarrassment of leaches, diet of worms) when no suitable collect could be found. He memorized the state birds and flowers of every state. For a while he was learning the scientific binomials of every mammal (*Lynx rufus* = bobcat, *Cryptoprocta ferox*, or ferocious secret arse, = the Madagascarian fossa), until he realized how many different hundreds of species of vole there were, and gave up. He memorized poems, and snatches from poems. The thing he was best at memorizing, though, was numbers. Phone numbers, locker combinations. He knew the social security numbers of everyone in his family and several not-even-very-close friends because they'd once left the wrong piece of paper lying around for a second or two.

The point is, the real point is that of course, *of course* Oscar had memorized that address in the wilds of Brooklyn—a "two-fare zone," subway to bus. Of course he had memorized the time, which was Tuesday late; so late that it was actually Wednesday early. He had only had a glance, but the glance had taken it all in, alongside the ominous words on the paper: *The Goblin Market.*

V.K. was already home and asleep when Oscar crawled into bed. His bleached tuxedo, which would never be returned, lay discarded on the bathroom floor.

And in the morning, the late morning, over pu-erh, V.K. asked about the night. What was there to say? Should he just tell V.K. about a secret and possibly forbidden Goblin Market in what was possibly a snuff brothel in Brooklyn? Should he admit that the punk kid who'd left his backpack in the kitchen was M.I.A.? How do you even start to explain how the throne of Satan got transported from Berlin to Moscow?

Instead Oscar, who'd been checking his email on V.K.'s laptop, said, "I just got a weird note from Susan Peters. It says '91.1' and '12:07' and today's date. 12:07 is in like half an hour."

"I think 91.1 is WFMU," said V.K.

Half an hour is not a long time when you have to determine whether you even own a radio any more, let alone work out how to configure an antenna and two coat hangers to receive the Jersey station. The ancient clock radio was playing (a piano) by 12:03, though, and two curious fellows, one of whom (V.K.) was really being a very good sport about the strangeness and the mystery, were listening.

"By special request," the D.J. said and the plinking and plunking had stopped, "we present an exclusive performance of Wink-Wink Theater for our friends from A—t."

"Does wink-wink mean it's gay?" asked V.K.

"Shhh!" said Oscar.

But what followed was simply short excerpts from three orchestral pieces without further jockey interference. First there was Wagner's wedding march from *Lohengrin*—V.K. had to identify the composer, although the tune was clear: "here comes the bride." That played for a couple of minutes, with an abrupt cutoff segueing to the opening everyone knows, the fate-knocks of Beethoven's *Fifth*. Less than a minute of Beethoven, and when that stopped there came an unrecognizable choral piece, which the D.J. cut off after five minutes or so and identified as *Hiawatha's Wedding Feast* by Samuel Coleridge-Taylor. That was the end of Wink-Wink Theater.

"What was that?" asked V.K.

"A riddle," said Oscar. "A riddle I do not understand. Is Samuel Coleridge-Taylor a clue?"

Well, anything might be a clue, but Samuel Coleridge-Taylor was not simply a mixed-up Samuel Taylor Coleridge. A moment of internet research revealed that he was a real composer, best known for *Hiawatha's Wedding Feast* (1898).

"So much for that idea," said Oscar.

"What did he mean by it being for our friends from A—t? Was that just you?"

"Maybe."

"How'd he know where you went to undergrad? Would Susan know? And he did say *friends* plural."

And there were a thousand other questions to be asked about this mysterious broadcast. Start with: Why wouldn't Peters just send an email?

They sat and thought, and then they got pencils and worked out possibilities and commonalities. All three pieces were nineteenth century, that dazzling century of marvels—one each from the beginning, middle, and end of the century. But the order was jumbled: 1850, 1808, 1898. What did this mean?

The radio, no help, was now playing Mahler, so they listened to Mahler.

Oscar replied to Peters's email with a "???"

And people went to libraries and people went to lunch, and life, to all appearances, continued normally. If there were secret laws governing the organization of the universe— Benford's law, governing distribution of digits in apparently

169

random numbers; or Zipf's law, governing the ratios of word frequencies in texts—well, these laws were all math, and Oscar was not to think of math. But secret laws required secret legislatures, did they not? And on this Oscar lay in bed and pondered. Who straightens the straight edge? Who measures the measuring cup? Who tunes the tuning fork?

They do.

· 26 · Clue-huntin' · Illus. Thomas Moran · An endless ride out · Bimulosity · Longwood Silver · The Goblin Market · Miscellaneous booths · Potential Mason Words; try rearranging them, maybe · The murder motive revealed · There was a veil past which etc. · Antimendacity ·

Tuesday rolled around, as it was going to. And then Tuesday dragged its belly towards dusk, which only took a thousand years subjective time.

Oscar did not even bother to make up a Union excuse. Instead he told V.K. he had an idea about the Peters riddle, and needed to do midnight reconnaissance.

"Take me with you, of course," said V.K.

"The next time I do something stupid, I will take you with me," said Oscar, "but this time I only know how to get one person in."

"Will I know eventually what kind of weird thing you're up to?" asked V.K.

"Definitely," Oscar lied, assuming he would if not tonight then sometime soon disappear, leaving only a ghost to haunt his old fiance, to spy over his shoulder as he read books, to knock the tea cup from his hand when he was about to drink it still too hot. A kind of benevolent but still destructive poltergeist might be a good afterlife.

"I used to have a car," said V.K., which in their private coded language meant *be careful*.

If Oscar and Peters had had a private coded language, they wouldn't even be in this mess. Oscar Cox imagined a future where everyday objects had to be spoken of in a riddling, paraphrastic way, as in kennings, or as in the *Alexandra* of Lycophron (ca. 250 B.C.). "That which keeps Ferwood Shorest from burning down," you would say instead of *firetruck*. "What it says on the tombstone of the king of England and Denmark," you would say instead of *canoe trip*. Everything was a clue.

(*Canute R.I.P.*, see?)

The subway trip from Queens to Brooklyn is so absurd that you might as well ride a bicycle, if you had one. But Oscar rode the subway. He read as he went, for research, a library copy of Longfellow's *Hiawatha* (1855). Something would fall in place.

Fiercely the red sun descending
Burned his way along the heavens,
Set the sky on fire behind him,
As war-parties, when retreating,
Burn the prairies on their war-trail;
And the moon, the Night-sun, eastward,
Suddenly starting from his ambush,
Followed fast those bloody footprints,
Followed in that fiery war-trail,
With its glare upon his features.

Was this a clue? Everything was a clue. It was nine when Oscar boarded the subway and it was after eleven when he got off the bus at the ass end of Brooklyn and started walking.

When Mary Shelley wants to get away with leaving out information she writes, chattily, "I see by your eagerness and the wonder and hope which your eyes express, my friend, that you expect to be informed of the secret with which I am acquainted; that cannot be." But then, Mary Shelley also writes (same page): "Remember, I am not recording the vision of a madman." The "remember" is what makes it good. Perhaps Mary Shelley has nothing to do with us. But nevertheless, we cannot reveal Oscar's secret route to the Goblin Market. What if Walter Pilkoç should read it?

The trees were uncharacteristically bare. It must have been somewhere in New York's ninth district, judging by all the Weiner signs hanging from fire escapes; or perhaps it was an extrazoned region unrepresented in Congress, and the Weiner signs meant something else.

May be he was there a little early. People were setting up booths in an empty lot that had clearly once been a parking lot before implacable nature had burst, here and there, and then in so many places, through the crumbling asphalt. There were peripheral standing sections of chain-link fence, twenty feet high, but there were not many of them. Oscar walked through the lot, then walked a block away and waited a little. All the day had been a dreary one at best, and dim, but the rain had resolved into a fine mist, now; everything was soggy. The sky, indeed, was like lace. Finally a man dressed as a pirate came up to him. "Seeking a new Korea?" the man asked.

"I beg pardon?" said Oscar.

"You seeking for a new Korea?" the man asked. As with most pirates of the Caribbean variety, with the eyepatch and the Jolly Roger hat, this ruddy-faced man did not appear to be Korean any more than he appeared to be Caribbean.

"I've never been to the old one, so it seems perverse to search for a newer version," said Oscar.

"*Ahhhhh!*" the man cried inexplicably, and Oscar quickly returned to the weedy parking lot. It was in a better state now. The booths sold hand-thrown pots, or baggies of artisanal fake vomit, or hot dogs. There was a juggler who only juggled invisible objects, perhaps very skillfully. Two hideous naked men walked by carrying an enormous fish. One of them was Lyndon LaRouche.

This was the place, all right. Whatever Oscar was going to learn he was going to learn tonight, or so he assumed. Reality would peel away like dryer's lint.

What did Oscar learn at the Goblin Market? The first thing he learned was about that statistic people quote, that New Yorkers eat on average two spiders a year—Oscar learned that was true. Not that most people ate two spiders; the *mode* was zero spiders; but the *mean* was two spiders; there's *this one guy*...

What did Oscar learn at the Goblin Market? He learned that you could build a flamethrower out of simple metal scraps and an old bellows, and you could then try to sell the flamethrower. You could also try (the same people tried) to sell a morphine-scented shampoo called Soapariffic!, and who knew which idea was worse?

What did Oscar learn at the Goblin Market? He learned, when the pirate guy reappeared, that said pirate guy was Bostonian, and had been trying to ask Oscar if he wanted *a new career*, a career on the high seas as a pirate. "Ahhhhh!" Once that was clear, Oscar said no, and the pirate went away. "Ahhhhh!" he said, as he left, like a pirate, a pirate from Boston.

What did Oscar learn at the Goblin Market? That ancient

wisdom is encoded in marginal places where no one had thought to erase it. This is where Oscar first heard of the "Jeck og Jill" rhyme from Anholt, Denmark; another example would be "Hickory Dickory Dock," which preserves the number sequence eight–nine–ten from an archaic counting system once used by British shepherds...

No one was talking about *They*. Everyone was talking about nursery rhymes. "'How Many Miles to Babylon' is when it really gets interesting," explained a man with a tube sticking out of his throat, and also a fez. Oscar did not catch his name, but he immediately and silently nicknamed him Tracheottoman, and then he was so vexed that he could not tell V.K. this witticism that he missed whatever the rhyme was about.

> ...of my threescore years and ten,
> Twenty will not come again...

But none of that *helped*. Someone played an accordion by a bonfire. Someone made origami animals you could buy for a quarter, for burning. A hare-lipped guitar-playing priest called Father Pick—

Pick?

Father Pick belonged to an order that took seriously Saul's name change to Paul upon converting, and he played guitar alongside many a Pichael and Pimothy and Partholemew. He himself, of course, was known as Pichard.

—had a complicated theory, conveyed partially in song, about how the crucifixion secretly reenacted the Lord's triumph over aquatic chaos monsters in the most ancient days (Ps. 74:13–14); instead of the Lord pinning a chaos monster to the ground, he pinned himself to the ground, and...

"And what about secret societies?" Oscar ventured asking him.

"Look, if that is about that stupid book with the short chapters, I want to make clear that any genuine exposé of the church would not be written in words of only one syllable."

"No," said Oscar, "I don't mean the Catholic Church (which I would say is too famous to be a genuine secret society). I mean the real secret guys. The ones with the Mason Word."

And Father Pick admitted he had heard of the Mason Word. As he understood it, the Mason Word was actually just four or five everyday words that rarely appeared in conjunction. *Prince, tree, child, book*, maybe. Mason Words, more like it. Only together did they have any power.

And what do they do?

It was chilly for the first week of August. Oscar walked from booth to booth, from strange event to strange event, asking. *What do they do?* Then he realized he wasn't sure if that was his primary question. Then he realized he wasn't sure what his primary question should be. *Where is Mordecai Johnson?* seemed overly specific.

"Hypothetically," Oscar asked some hoary cripple with malicious eye who looked like he knew what he was doing, "if some secret society—one of the really big ones—wanted someone dead who was not in a rival secret society, why would they want it? What would they be after?"

The guy who looked like he knew what he was doing said, "You have to understand that any self-respecting secret society is playing a game on several boards at once. Whatever move they make will have to be valid and helpful against more than one opponent. Maybe they want this dude dead, but more likely they simply just don't not want this dude dead, and they'll sacrifice a pawn to get their other pieces in a better position."

"But let's say this guy was going to make a big announcement..."

"It's unlikely an announcement would look big to any of these groups," said the guy who looked like he knew what he was doing. "But the announcement might look big to *us*, and maybe sacrificing a loud and showy pawn would keep us from being distracted from what they want us to see."

"Wait. Did you say, 'what they want us to see' or 'what *They* want us to see'?"

"What's the difference?"

"Hang on. Are *They* even that famous if you're not at a special event made up entirely of people obsessed with them?"

"I don't know how to answer that sentence."

If no one had heard of *They*, did that make them a successful secret society, or a rinky-dink unsuccessful secret society?

People rode by on unicycles (cliché) and people drove by in an antique wood-fired steam tractor, lovingly restored (somewhat odder). Not everyone was in a wild-eyed frenzy to exhume whatever secret answer to their ill-formed questions was lying just beneath the broken asphalt, if only some treasure map would reveal where. Some people seemed to be having fun. There was a bit of a carnival atmosphere, in a Boschy, cat-walking-on-its-hind-legs way. Someone might have had the face of an ape, or possibly was actually an ape. A man detached his head. A woman blew cigar smoke out of her tear ducts. Remember, I am not recording the vision of a madman.

Totar tarsinat er trifor tarsinater tuscer naharcer iabuscer nomner nerf sihitu ansihitu iouie hostatu anhostatu tursitu tremitu hondu holtu ninctu nepitu sonitu sauitu preplotatu preuilatu...

176

Who was that over by the all-you-can-eat marshmallow tent? Was that Miss Jones? No; impossible; Jones did not wear mustachios, did she? False alarm.

The hopheads and the shambloids seemed to congregate over at one side of the parking lot. They lolled on the damp asphalt and chewed on the protruding weeds. "Hothera, dothera, dick," one said. He had only three teeth in his mouth, and none of them were fastened to his gums. He just swished the three back and forth between his cheeks like sourballs.

And behind him was a strange tent, a tent with a veil before the entrance. A sinister-looking man in a mauve vest stood before the veil, stood so still that Oscar thought he might be a wax statue, and, stepping carefully over the prone humans and their scattered effluvia, Oscar Cox approached.

The man moved his head only, as he looked Oscar up and down.

"Hello," said Oscar, but the man was already saying, in a thick, halting voice,

"You may not enter."

"Perhaps we could talk this—"

"You may not enter."

The pirate was walking by, and said, cheerfully, as Oscar slunk away "Buck up, me hottie."

"What? Oh right," said Oscar.

"I can get you in, if that's what you really want. Five sixths of piracy is just knowing the shibboleth that will gain you entrance pretty much any place. Avast!" And maybe Oscar made some vague promises of adventures on the bounding main; maybe the pirate was just a very helpful, or even suspiciously helpful, guy. In any event, the pirate went up to the tent and said, "Ahhhhh! *Let the wattas be potted.*"

177

"You may not enter."

The pirate walked away, shaking his head with grudging (as they say) respect. "Wicked cunning. They got a deaf man at the daw, ain't no shibboleth in the lexicon that'll get him to open it."

So there was that then. Oscar Cox was pure of heart and rolling in knowledge and bearing the imprimatur of the week-end's charity ball and a shibboleth from the Scourge of the Southies. He was even a virgin. But he may not enter.

There were voices from inside the tent, and flickering lights. Someone was laughing.

Eventually, hours later, people began breaking down the booths, but when Oscar went back to the mystery booth, it was already gone. He first *felt*, then reified that into *knew* that he had missed some opportunity and failed in his quest. The final signpost on the trail had pointed to nothing more.

As he began his long walk back to where the buses were no longer running, and then the longer walk beyond, he realized that he had not even told, his whole time in Brooklyn, one overt lie. Somewhere behind his eyes a sphincter dilated and the salty humors began to ease out.

· 27 · Short chapter, very appealing · Anabasis · Secrets of the dawn · The legacy of Samuel Morse · Samuel Coleridge-Taylor and the Mystery of the Final Clue · Case closed ·

What did the Mason Word do? Did it let you (as the guitar-priest finally suggested) remake the world?

Ah, Love! could thou and I with Fate conspire

To grasp this sorry Scheme of Things entire!
Would not we shatter it to bits—and then
Re-mould it nearer to the Heart's Desire!

Nietzsche said we should love the world just as it is however it is, but (as some have pointed out) "that is really hard to do and Nietzsche died in the nuthatch like Percy Crosby." Anyone else is probably going to want to change things. Would Oscar, if he had it, the Mason Word that is, not change some things?

What are the things of the world? "Dritte, gile, and wanite," the old poem says: shit, guile, and vanity. Could this not be improved on?

Ah, but not just anyone can use the Mason Word (again, so sang the priest in loose fourteeners). He who is not prepared for it—through purification, or spiritual exercise, or mere congenital Coast-Guardy/Scouty readiness—hears but sounding brass, or a tinkling cymbal. These are the priest's examples, of course. To him, the unprepared, the chaff, the preterite, the Mason Word is nothing.

"It's like a surprise," the priest had said. "It's like a joke. Would you laugh if I told you Why did the chicken cross the road?"

"Of course not," Oscar had said.

"Have you ever laughed at the joke?"

"Probably not," admitted Oscar. "It's always been a joke in the background. I grew up hearing parodies of it, but no one tells that joke seriously."

"You must have heard it for the first time when you were too young to understand it, when you were too young to understand jokes, because all of us did. And so we'll never get to laugh at it. Now, not all of his have heard the Word. In the beginning was the Word, but most have us have never heard it spoken. If you hear the Word the way you heard the chicken joke, well...it would be spoiled forever."

"And that would be it? It'd be useless, then?" Oscar had asked him.

You can, it turns out, shrug while paying guitar. Key of G, and all simple chords. "That would be it, but I don't know *useless*. I guess you could go around telling it to people you didn't like. Ruin it for them. If you're a spoiler."

Who would be a spoiler? Well, not one Oscar Cox, apparently. Not because he did not want revenge, and not even because he was not worthy, of course, but simply because he no longer had any ideas of where to find this Word; or where to find anything along the banks of this underground stream. The remaining facts that had looked like clues—7^{2^2}, an anagrammed *et in Arcadia* etc., etc.—didn't make the least bit of sense. He had nothing.

The sun was just starting its bloody footprints up when a sleepy and despondent Oscar struggled home. He remembered the line from E. Nesbit's *Five Children and It* (1902), and whispered: "I wish we were all as beautiful as the day."

V.K. was still asleep, but as Oscar crawled into bed he stirred, and rolled over, and with his lips right against Oscar's ear whispered: That he'd been thinking about the Peters Program. That ("as you know") he was once a ham radio aficionado, and he was aware, at least in part because of his fist initial, at least in part because it was famously used in WWII as the call sign for Victory, that Beethoven's Fifth was also dit dit dit da the Morse code for *V*.

"Al Gore," murmured Oscar sleepily.

So then (V.K. continued, in a whisper) he started wondering

if the other tunes were also Morse code. And indeed da da dit da here comes the bride was Q.

Q. V. But what Coleridge-Taylor's piece spelled was beyond him, sorry, all he got.

Oscar was suddenly wide awake. "I forgot to brush my teeth," he said, which was at least true, and while V.K. sprawled back into slumber, he slipped into their living room, pulled a dictionary off the shelf. His heart beat a trochaic Lönnrot rhythm as he flipped through the pages. Under *M, quod vide*, it provided every Morse code letter.

"Aha!" he said out loud. "Oscar Cox has solved the case!"

Sleepily, from the bedroom, came the question, "Did you just refer to yourself in the third person?"

"No, of course not," said Oscar Cox. "You must have been dreaming."

· 28 · **Come on, get involved!** · **The knowledge** · **It was badly done, indeed!** · **Same old ambages** · **Whim-whams** · **Face eaten by rats** · **One last mission** ·

So the mystery was solved, but unfortunately, the solution made very little sense; or rather the solution was at best a clue pointing towards another clue, but Oscar had no way to follow up without a car. He started saving nickels for a bus ticket.

And things returned, more or less to normal. Our boys sweated through the summer, but the library was air conditioned, and at night, with the windows open, a foul but cooling breeze blew in from the river. Oscar was not sure what to do with his time, so he tried looking to books for advice. He knew that patriotism, according to Emerson, was the last refuge

181

of the scoundrel. He also knew that violence, according to Asimov, was the first refuge of the incompetent. Oscar took out his datebook and wrote "violence" in the morning and "patriotism" in the evening, and figured he'd wing the parts in between. For Oscar had the knowledge but he had no way of doing anything about it, which, if he wanted to, he could have said was a metaphor for his whole life. Ha ha ha, he would have to say, after he said it, if he said it.

"Do you know what Humpty Dumpty is?" Oscar asked V.K. over supper.

Humpty Dumpty is an egg.

"But how do you know Humpty is an egg?" Oscar asked. The rhyme doesn't say so. Was it some stray Kate Greenaway or Beatrix Potter illustration? The *Looking-Glass* cameo? Or the force of folk wisdom, pseudo-Jungian, secretly transmitting secret knowledge through secret conduits? "Not-egg," "not-egg," "not-egg," we tell the children, and the children manage to hear "egg"?

And this was the closest Oscar came to revealing to the household what he had learned at the Goblin Market.

Then one morning he got a call from someone who was probably Mr. Pizzoli-with-a-falsetto purporting to be Mr. Pizzoli's secretary and demanding Oscar come to his office on Wednesday. Oscar looked at a calendar to see how many weeks had passed since the Goblin Market night, how many weeks upon weeks he had lived the life of a normal man. The answer was one.

"I knew that," said Oscar.

He rode the train down to N— Y— U. Oscar had started reading through V.K.'s bookshelves instead of trying to figure out, on his own, what stupid books to read; and somewhere around Union Square he came across, in *Emma* (1815), the scene when Knightly tells Emma that she should endure tedious and dull people if they are good and decent.

"Could this be true?" sputtered Oscar. "Have I wasted my whole life?" But the next stop was his. He marched, as to his death, towards the bowels of the psych building. Another day, another labyrinth. The sign of the door of the office of Erica Jones had been replaced by a sign for the office of Arsenio Moorcock, and Oscar barely even looked that way. Too much, too much. The only question was whether Johnson's escape would get Oscar chewed out, or actually murdered. He probably should have gotten his house in order if he was going to get murdered. He probably should have told his fiance the solution to all things. He probably should have finished *Emma*.

The same old ambages, and there was Pizzoli's office. "Will Peters's mysterious secret die with me?" was the last thing Oscar said before he caught Pizzoli's eye, and there was the sound of shot.

"My boy, it was splendidly done!" Pizzoli said. In his hand was a foaming bottle of champagne, which he poured out parsimoniously into a styrofoam cup. "Why do you look so sick?"

"The banjos. The whim-whams. Bender last night, you understand," said Oscar, who understood nothing, but resented the cliché. And yet he took the offered cup, while Pizzoli swigged—swug?—from the bottle.

"Officially," Pizzoli said, "we'll just say he was caught in a rat tide. Most of the" (he glanced at a cheat sheet hidden somewhere on his desk) "soft tissues were eaten away. We could only really recognize him by the conference badge in his pocket."

Oscar went to take his hat off and place it over his heart, but of course he was not wearing a hat. "Was it—did it look like a quick death?"

"Sure, sure," said Mr. Pizzoli. "The coroner's one of ours, he'll suppress the bullets, the" (cheat sheet) "ten bullets."

"Right," said Oscar. "First the bullets, then the rats." In death we are animals, and it is exposed, our fantasy that we were more. We are meat and blood.

"Get him cremated right away. The coroner said—" and here Mr. Pizzoli seemed to weigh his words carefully, so as not to give offense. "He said that the bullets' pattern was slipshod, like someone firing pointblank in a panic. Like an...*amateur.*"

"Of course," said Oscar. "In case a less sympathetic coroner found the body, it would hardly do to let him deduce a professional was behind things. Two to the heart, one to the head—it'd be like a signature."

"Of course," said Mr. Pizzoli, barely refilling the bottom part of Oscar's cup. The styrofoam where Pizzoli had held it started to liquefy and bubble away, for he was like a hamburger and left a grease stain on everything he touched. "I told him the same thing. Now, do you still have the gun?"

"Naturally I tossed it off the deck of the Staten Island ferry. Anything else would have been foolish."

"Yes, well. We'll have De & De take the cost of it off your next check, of course." You will have already guessed that this was the real name of the construction company. "And that about wraps things up."

"Is the strike over?"

"Oh, no. No, no, no, no. No. Oh, but there is one more thing. A smidge awkward, maybe. The boy's family—well, we're mailing most of his ashes to Colorado, but I guess it's

184

tradition for some of them to be sent back to his frat to be buried in their herb garden. We'll provide a lovely urn, at no cost to you, and it all should be ready in a couple of days."

There was the kind of silence that Oscar felt was supposed to mean something, but he also felt it would be gauche to talk more about killing Johnson, now that they had progressed to burying him, and he didn't know what else to talk about.

"An urn," he prompted.

"Yes, for you to deliver. The Union told me your fraternity brothers requested it special. A personal touch really means the world, don't you think?"

"Could I," asked Oscar, "borrow a car?"

"Of course not."

And Oscar almost said, "Then how in God's green earth am I going to get to Massachusetts?" but then instead he said, imaginary hat over imaginary heart, "I will deliver the ashes, no problem. It will be a great honor."

• 29 •**The king is dead** • **Alternate versions** • **Fan-favorite Peters's swan song** • **Catacombs and honeycombs** • **Heliogen** • **Dr. Sir William Withey Gull** •

Oscar considered (since he was already downtown) detouring to the Rufus Library, where V.K. would probably be now. But instead he headed home, plotting things out his whole subway ride. All the pieces, or what few he had left with Johnson off the board, were now in place. "Check," he said, first to the world and second to *They* and finally to you, the reader, whoever you are. But this was the time he feared he would blow it. "Check." But the one thing Oscar could not bring himself to do was mate.

185

He wondered what he would learn in A—t, and he wondered, if the time came when he told this tale to others, if he would pretend like it had been his idea. "Well, Mr. Pizzoli, I'll pay for your gun, but there's one requirement. I must personally deliver etc." Swell music, cut scene.

He was back in Astoria and most of the way home when a door opened up in a solid brick wall and Peters stepped out. She was wearing goggles. "Oscar I've been looking all over for you," she said. The door was gone now; perhaps a trick of the light it had been.

"I've—ditto. I've learned a lot."

"I've learned so much. You wouldn't believe the things I've seen. Did you figure out my message?"

"Yes but why—"

"No! No! Don't say it out loud! And look, look, I want to hear everything you've been doing in the last week, but I also have things to tell you. I don't know how much time we have. People keep asking me if I know who Jack the Ripper is, and if I say no I'm an illiterate moron, and if I say yes I'm concealing the identity of a murderer, and I'm not falling for that one! I've got to tell you. You know how like ten years ago, people who'd already been saying 'between you and I' started never saying *me* at all? It's not an accident, it's part of *They*'s war on the objective case. Soon enough if you ask someone: 'Have you heard about *They*?' it'll sound just like: 'Have you heard about they?' which will be how people say: 'Have you heard about them?' And all anyone will say is: 'They who?' And then how will we talk about any of this?" She was breathless. She was exhilarated. She was nonstop. "Do you know about the tunnel?"

"I know about *some* tunnels, yes," said Oscar with admirable

186

precision. "Should you hide in my apartment?"

"First place they'd look. Just step here out of the light, out of the satellite..." They were under an awning now, on the front stoop of some random apartment. "Last week, no a week and a half ago, let me tell you. I was out on Long Island, following up a lead, and my source was driving, and she drove into a warehouse, it looked like an abandoned warehouse, and down a ramp, and then through a really long tunnel, and we came out in Bridgeport, Connecticut."

"There's a tunnel under the Sound?" Oscar incredulated.

"There's a tunnel under the Sound. But get this. Next day I tried to Google it. And I was in the search engine, and I typed 'secret tunnel between Port Jefferson and—' and it wouldn't type any more. It erased the whole thing. I could type almost anything, but anything about this tunnel, even a paraphrase, in English or Spanish—I couldn't type it. You can't even type 'subsonic tunnel,' no joke. I don't just mean Google, I mean the computer literally would not register the words. Not in an email, not in a Word doc. It might change *tunnel* to *ferry*, or it might delete the whole thing." Peters was sunburned and manic. Her feet were long, her eyes were light, and her hair was wild. Actually, her eyes—she had just removed the goggles, they were aviator goggles—were wild, too. She was bursting, brimming with the excitement. There was a still-unhealed cut running over he left eye and up into her hairline.

"Just in English and Spanish?"

"What do I speak besides English and Spanish?" she said. "I only know dirty words in Japanese. But the point is there are tunnels like this *everywhere*. There are secret catacombs and honeycombs and in the old days, I mean like ten years ago, you'd never get away with this. Word would spread, and the secret tunnel wouldn't be secret any more. But now you can't spread the word. I tried getting an old cassette recorder and recording information about the tunnel under the Sound, and it worked fine. But when I used my digital recorder, it wouldn't record. You can say it on an analog phone line, but you can't say it on a cell phone, or even on a digital phone line. If you see more Voice over IP phone services coming up in the next year or so—well, you'll never be able to talk about tunnels on those."

"But not just tunnels?"

"Now you understand why I couldn't just come out and email you! I cashed in a favor with a DJ I knew. But that was over a week ago. I've learned about four hundred thousand things since then. Do you know about fractional elements, like the elements between hydrogen and helium? Do you know what you can build with them?"

"Even with my dim understanding of chemistry I know that there can be no element between hydrogen and helium," said Oscar patiently.

"Well, not if you limit your atomic numbers to whole numbers," said Peters, still brimming. "And some of the things you can build with betweenium—I have it all set up, a way to circumvent their stupid strictures, no codes needed."

"A way to—"

"Yes! I've managed to set up several invisible broadcast towers on crypto-ley lines..."

"Frito Lay what?"

"Pay attention, Oscar! This is important. Tomorrow night the word gets out. Everything is set to override the airwaves. On Thursday Mulciber and Proserpina will be in alignment. Uranus will be in Pisces."

Oscar almost said *Man, you've said a mouthful! nyuck nyuck!*, but a glance silenced him.

"Everyone will know," she continued, busting with pride, as though she were the hero, as though Oscar Cox were some ancillary character in the continuing adventures of Susan "Scoop" Peters, blimp-rider, scorpion-tamer, devil-may-care badass fujoshi. (*Badass Fujoshi* is a probable title of the work.) "The truth is, everything that you know and a good half of what I know will be public in a little over twenty-four hours."

"Should you be telling me this? Shouldn't you be in hiding?"

One lock of hair kept falling, wantonly, into her pan, and she puffed her cheeks to blow it back into place. She was having a good time. "It's all set up already. I could die right now and the message would still go out. And I have secret subsidiary transmitters set up in Detroit, in Ottawa, all over the place. There's no way to find them all in this kind of time frame."

Just then the apartment door opened and a man with a clipboard strolled through. "Excuse me," he said, "do you know who Jack the Ripper is?"

Peters dopplered out, "Thursday! Turn on your radio or non-cable television," as she vaulted over the stoop's stone banister, landed in a shadowy place behind a trash can, turned sideways, and then turned sideways *once more*, somehow, and was gone. She will not appear again.

"I've heard of him, yes, but I don't know his identity," said Oscar.

• 30 • The Mason Word •

A lot of things happened on Wednesday night and Thursday

morning—Oscar double checked the radio set up, and he washed his socks, and he read two-thirds (penance for his sins) of *Silas Marner* (1861)—but there's no point in artificially drawing out suspense by enumerating them in detail. Unless you are the kind of reader who plows through a chapter a night, setting the book down responsibly on the nightstand come close of "...said Oscar" and dreaming all night, and anticipating all day, you will not be held in suspense. On that Thursday, August 14, 2003, the largest power failure in this hemisphere's history plunged the continent, from Ontario to Maryland, into darkness.

"It's terrorists!" several people screamed as they ran through the streets of Astoria in a bathrobe or a patrolman's uniform. But most people failed to panic or loot and simply sweated and endured. Oscar was at home, like Moses, when the lights went out, sitting by the still and silent appliances, but V.K. had to make the long and crowd-choked walk up Manhattan and across the Triborough Bridge. He was full of stories of generous hot dog vendors and C-list celebrities who directed traffic or handed out waters.

The night was dark and long. The city that never, slept. Piecemeal the lights came on again, and if your anus was still in pieces—well, who knew? Oscar sat by his radio and his little black-and-white leporaural television that weekend, just in case. The lights flickered on and then off and then on for good, but no revelations came over the airwaves. Budd Dwyer and Christine Chubbuck didn't reunite for one last legendary on-air interview.

Whatever the frequency was, Kenneth wasn't telling. "Scoop" Peters did not appear again.

And then, on Tuesday, the urn arrived in the mail, which

seemed a weird way to go about things. I mean, if you were going to put the urn in the mail anyway, why not send it...?

But Oscar was going to hand-deliver. It was a romantic, sentimental beau geste, and no one could resist it. V.K. could not resist it. He was even willing to call in the Schwartz. Schwartz still had a car.

Schwartz couldn't or wouldn't get off work, so it would have to be a weekend. On Saturday morning they gathered at Schwartz's apartment, and waited as Schwartz assembled supplies for the six-hour round-trip drive: Meteor–brand ("it's meatier!") beef jerky, a bunch of bananas, three ice waters in three thermoi for the riders. This last took time. Schwartz had read somewhere that hot water freezes faster than cold, and so, invariably, whenever he made ice he would first boil the water and then pour it from the kettle into the ice cube tray. The plastic tray had been melted and refrozen so many times that the ice, when he pried it out, was not in the shape of cubes but rather in the shape of tortured dwarves, or ginger root. But getting it out, this was the problem. While Schwartz sweated and groaned over the implacably wedged ice dwarves, Oscar snooped around the apartment, planning on looking at the bookshelves but finding none.

"Gravy! but you have a lot of capes!" he said by the coat rack. But he had to be nice. Schwartz was his ride.

Everyone made one last pit stop in the bathroom. V.K. swung the door ~93% shut with no hesitation, and indeed it was closed enough that the sounds of micturition were barely audible. As he exited, Oscar did not say anything, and V.K. did not say anything, but the expression on his face said: *What do you want from me? I finally figured it out.*

And then the endless drive began. Schwartz refused to speed

on the highway, regardless of what lane he was in, which was not so bad in and of itself, despite the horns honking behind and around him and the people who tried, but failed, to spit on his car as they passed on the right; but he also talked non-stop about the virtue he accrued by not speeding.

"It doesn't even save you much time, this lawlessness," he opined. "You could be doing a buck ten down the I-95, how much sooner would you reach your destination than an honest man, just following the speed limit? Almost no time at all!"

"You'd get there twice as fast," said Oscar from the back seat. V.K. was shotgun, the urn between his knees.

"No, that can't be right," said Schwartz.

"I'm not really supposed to do math, but this is so very basic that I couldn't help—" But Oscar stopped, because he had to be nice. And then, a few miles later, the speed limit increased to 65, and it turned out his math was off, anyway.

To change the topic, Schwartz began complaining repeatedly about every single thing north, and by extension east, of New York City. The trees they drove by. The hicks they did not see, but who were doubtless around. The lack of rest stops. "What if we have to go to the bathroom?" he said, with a rhetorical hand-flourish.

"We'll just have to take Richard II's advice," V.K. suggested, with a bit of a Conneryesque burr. *Advishe.*

Schwartz scratched his head, simian-style, but Oscar pieced it together, and said: "For God's sake let us shit upon the ground." He did not laugh, but he grinned and when V.K. looked back and caught his eye he, too was grinning. He couldn't help it.

They drove on; and all around them, the greenery of enemy territory.

192

"What would you guys say," Oscar asked at last, "if I mentioned there was a chance that Mordecai Johnson, A—t undergrad, is not in the urn, but is in fact alive, because he was carrying a gun on him and he killed someone who wanted to kill him, whoever that was, whose face was eaten by rats? And now the rat-eaten guy in in the urn and Mordecai Johnson is living some kind of secret underground life, possibly of debauchery, possibly just literally underground?"

"This is in very poor taste," Schwartz said, but V.K. said,

"Unlikely things that are comforting are still unlikely."

Oscar's book was in his bag, which was in the trunk, and reading the only text around, the ingredients off a Meteor Jerky wrapper (filler; unspecified protein source) was inadvisable. Furthermore, Schwartz's car radio was broken, so that it could not turn off nor could the volume be lowered. Schwartz hated all forms of music, but he knew of a radio station for people with exactly this malfunction, which broadcast only silence, and he kept the radio tuned in to that FM band. In the mountains, though, the station started to cut out, and loud static filled the car. (It was only at this point that Schwartz was forced to explain about the radio and the special FM station.)

"This station with silence," said Oscar from the back. "That's a pretty obscure thing to know about."

"I heard about it somewhere," said Schwartz.

Oscar's suspicions were aroused. "Do you know anything about tunnels?"

"I never drive through tunnels. I'm a bridge man."

"Does the word *They* mean anything to you?"

"They who?"

V.K. suggested that they look for a radio station with inoffensive music, but Schwartz swore there was no such creature, so it was static up 91, static pulling into the town of A—t. Oscar could endure it, though, because for the first time in weeks, he was fairly sure that he was not about to be killed either accidentally by fratboys or on purpose by Union goons. He wasn't *sure* sure, but he thought the odds were now in his favor.

Likely something might kill him, but probably not goons or fratboys.

The car stopped in front of the familiar decaying architecture of ΣΩΔ house, and only when he shut off the car was there blessed silence.

"Thank you for the ride," Oscar said into the enormous void left by the retreating noise.

They all got out of the car, first to stretch their legs, then to get on with their mission, which, Oscar, of course, understood differently than the others. He had the knowledge. Schwartz was merely stretching his legs, stretching his neck, and looking around. It was mostly deserted on this noonish weekend, only one car parked nearby.

"'Intimate Apparel?'" Schwartz asked, reading from the storefronts across the street.

"'We put the mensch in unmentionables,'" V.K. suggested immediately, as though the whole world was just a grid, just a series of straight lines.

Bangs on the Sigma door got no answer. It was locked, and there didn't seem to be anyone in it. Oscar was carrying the urn, and it was surprisingly heavy.

"Maybe you can just leave it on the doorstep," Schwartz suggested. "Like baby Moses."

Moses, Moses. Was everything a clue? But V.K. stepped back to survey the street. There was no one around, and only that one car, smack in front of Strong's Feather Boas

Boutique; so he ducked in there and came out with an older woman in a turquoise tracksuit. She had apple cheeks so-called and glasses with frames so large and so red that you barely noticed her overblown Midwestern accent (not reproduced here). Her name, emblazoned on a My Name Is clip-on badge, was Mrs. Marit Minge, pronounced *ming-y*, to rhyme with *thingy*. "You're the fellow with the ashes?" she asked. "So tragic, so tragic."

"Rats are a real problem in today's urban existence," said Oscar. "So. Where is everyone?"

"It's the end of August; they all went home. No one's going to keep a house open over the summer. I look after things while they're gone usually, a bit of the den mother in me. They were expecting you last week, actually, before they had to go."

"I couldn't get off work," Schwartz said so quickly that Oscar wondered if he was lying.

"Well, what's done is done. They'll be back in September. I can bring the ashes in later if you want to leave them with me."

"Actually," Oscar said carefully, "I am supposed to bring it in myself. It's the code of the ΣΩΔomites. Very sacred."

"Well, I can open the door for you then," said Mrs. Minge obligingly. And she did. "Just put it anywhere."

The house was every bit as dilapidated as Oscar remembered, although someone had gone through the effort of collecting all the Solo cups and beer cans that had littered the stained and filthy floors, and stuffing them into trash bags. The effort had not extended to tying up or removing said trash bags, which lay on their sides in the hall, spilling their contents lazily out before them.

"Actually," Oscar said carefully, "I am supposed to bring the ashes to the goat room."

195

"The goat room? I don't like the sound of that," clucked Mrs. Minge, but Oscar said,

"Fan out, boys. Look for a secret staircase."

"Do what now?" said Schwartz.

"You know. Tap on the paneling, listen for a hollow spot. We'll find it."

"Oh, did you mean this goat room?" asked Mrs. Minge, toggling a secret catch under the wainscoting. A section of wall slid open.

"Now we're cooking," said Oscar. With gas, the four of them went down the stairs. At the final step, though, the light of triumph went out of Oscar's eyes. Everything looked right— the same posters were up. The same ballpoint nipples. The beer womb hunkered up against one wall. The stains on the floor all looked genuine.

"This is not the room," said Oscar.

"You've been here before?" V.K. asked.

"I was blindfolded on the way in and out, so I didn't know where the entrance was. But there were fourteen steps down to the genuine goat room, and only thirteen to this one." He moved forward and tugged one poster off the wall, just in case. There was nothing written on the back, nothing behind it. "Gentlemen, back upstairs. We'll find this place eventually."

Mrs. Minge's face was an inscrutable study. Schwartz, on the other hand, looked so put out that Oscar suggested the poor man guard the urn while the other two, we other two, tapped for secret doors. The first floor of the house was not so large, and the second secret catch was not so very hard to find. Another piece of wall, another down staircase.

"Oh my!" said Mrs. Minge.

Who could resist counting the stairs on the way down this

196

time? Fourteen later, Oscar stood in the old familiar room with the old familiar smells.

"You left the urn upstairs," Mrs. Minge said.

"We won't need it," said Oscar.

Schwartz's faint voice drifted plaintively from above: "Where did you guys go? Hello? Hello?"

"Technically no one is supposed to be in this room without a representative from National."

"You know an awful lot about this frathouse," Oscar said to Mrs. Minge as he approached the *QVC 100-Product Showdown* poster. It was hung low, so the bottom edge almost touched the filthy carpet.

"As I said, I look after things."

Oscar reached out and patted the poster. It made a loud slapping sound. "There's an empty space behind it," Oscar said. He turned around to see if Mrs. Minge was about to shoot him.

But instead it was just Schwartz, coming down the stairs and looking slightly more confused than usual. "An empty space?" he asked. "Another secret room? How did you know all this stuff?"

Oscar did not start with *I'm glad you asked that question* but went right to: "Peters's musical queues. V.K. got me Q and V and the only remaining clue was from *The Song of Hiawatha*."

"I have no idea what any of that means," Schwartz said.

"Wasn't it *Hiawatha's Wedding Feast*?" V.K. said.

"Yes, but *Hiawatha's Wedding Feast* is one-third of *The Song of Hiawatha*. Don't Encyclopedia Brown me. I looked it up. The point is that it's based on Longfellow's poem. And the clue has nothing to do with the music, really, which is less tedious than Longfellow's driving rhythm. Have you read Longfellow's

Hiawatha?"

"I don't think anyone reads that anymore," V.K. said.

"It's all in trochaic tetrameter. *Da* dit *da* dit, *da* dit *da* dit. Recognize that?"

"It's *C C*. Two *C*s," said V.K., who ("as you know") was once a ham radio aficionado, his childhood set still gathering dust in his parents' house.

"QVC C," said Oscar. "The Roman numeral C. Ergo: QVC 100, the 100-product showdown."

"So what's behind it?" Schwartz, who had been following very little, asked. Behind the poster, he meant.

"I have no idea," Oscar said and pulled the poster down from the top. Behind it was a three-foot tall entrance to a tunnel.

"You're not one of *They*, are you?" asked Mrs. Minge, while Schwartz nodded appreciatively that at least someone around here could use pronouns like a grownup. "Or the Bauxite Aluminati? The Society of the Nights of Eternal Levity? The W.C.T.U.?"

"Certainly not," said Oscar. "We're independent contractors."

She seemed to look Oscar over, and her eyes went through him utterly, like a spear. Perhaps she looked at all three of them. At last: "Well, I might as well show you the way," Mrs. Minge said. "Won't do for you boys to get lost, and anyway I'm the shortest one here." She ducked into the tunnel.

"So you do know the way," Oscar said, still in the room.

"I never denied it. I haven't told you any lies; I do look after the place when everyone's gone."

"You said you didn't know where the goat room is."

"I said I didn't like the sound of that, *goat room*, and that was true. Certainly there are some of us who don't refer to it as the goat room. It is the most sacred place in the whole house."

"Did you say *secret* or *sacred?*" asked Oscar.

"I said *sacred*, but many people get the two confused." She still had her keys in her hand, and she used a key-chain flashlight to illuminate the tunnel. There were plenty of rats, and plenty of rat droppings, and the occasional dried skeleton, its charred bones marred by a thousand little rodent nibbles. "Those boys are a handful, I can tell you. I'm the one who uncorked that freezer you were drowning in, you know. I had to use an Incan lever and some yogic techniques to move that fool thing. And when I heard you'd be coming back with the ashes, I furnished the decoy room with a duplicator ray. Much less sacred, that other basement. Thought it would keep you from coming in, from crossing over." She was huffing her way down the tunnel.

"I knew she was too poorly dressed to work at a feather boa boutique!" Schwartz hissed as he followed.

"Shhhh!"

Oscar felt a great weariness settle upon him, such weariness that he only with great effort forced his feet forward to follow the woman. Certainly he was too weary to describe what was happening himself. His withered guide led him along several obscure passages, with various windings to deceive the eye, and finally undid a door, through which, as it was opened, there came the sight and sound of rustling leaves.

But there were no leaves in the room, just columns. Column after column, extending, like funhouse mirrors, into infinity. A slight breeze wafted among them. Diffuse light with no discernible source filled the room. The columns looked like marble, but the veins were blue, like living things' veins, and it was possible they very slightly pulsated. Someone had

199

scratched somewhere *Abramowitz is a neo-classicist.* On the ground were a few skulls and fragments of bone, swept up into neat piles.

As the group passed between the columns, the pulsation became a sudden throb, and no one disintegrated.

"Well, you're not agents of any secret organization," said Mrs. Minge. "So that's a relief." Perhaps she meant that she was the one had to sweep up.

"Where are we?" asked Schwartz.

"We're under the B.P.O.E. lodge now. Maybe you'd like to refresh yourself in the garden?"

"Wait a moment," Oscar said. "B.P.O.E., that's..."

"The Benevolent and Protective Order of Elks. The Elks' Lodge," confirmed Mrs. Minge. "It's right across the way."

And "Mate!" cried Oscar, the way Stalky would have cried *fids*, the way Whitman would have cried *captain*. "Mate, O mate!" There was no echo in the enormous room. Everyone was looking at him. "What we'd like," said Oscar, "since you ask, is the Mason Word."

"Hard cheese," said Mrs. Minge.

But Oscar was not going to be stymied a second time. "Let the waters be parted," he said.

"What are you talking about?" asked Mrs. Minge, looking annoyed.

And it took a few more tries, but finally he hit upon, "Let the warters be potted," which made less sense, but perhaps good password123!s aren't supposed to make sense. Mrs. Minge sighed.

"Who asks for the Mason Word receives it," she said, "but I certainly don't recommend anything of the sort."

"Fine, fine, what's the word?"

"I'm sure I don't know. I can take you to it, but it's really not a good idea."

"Why is it not a good idea?" asked V.K., breaking his long and contemplative silence.

"You have to understand, the Mason Word can give someone who's ready for it understanding. Power. Enlightenment, some might call it. But very few are ready for it. The words are a surprise, and they can shock a prepared soul out of the conventional forms of thinking. That's not a very good way of describing it, but I don't have the words, really, the vocabulary. But almost no souls are prepared, you know."

"Right, I've heard about this," said Oscar. "Are you saying if you're not ready and you hear it you go Lovecraft-mad, Renfield-mad? Is that the idea?"

"Heavens, no! If you're not ready it won't work on you, that's all."

Oscar nodded. "That doesn't sound so bad."

Mrs. Minge's pan took on a stern, even frowning expression. *This is serious business, young man*, her pan said. "It's like a joke, though, isn't it? Imagine I told you Why did the chicken cross the road?"

"Please, I have this part down," said Oscar. "I heard the joke when I was too young for jokes."

"I know this one," said Schwartz, relieved at last. "To get to the other side."

Mrs. Minge nodded, and not at Schwartz. "That joke will never work on you. You'll never laugh, because laughter needs—"

"—a sudden conception," said V.K. It sounded like he was quoting someone. Maybe I'll look it up later.

"We all dream," said Mrs. Minge, "of one day hearing the

Word and watching everything we have ever misunderstood fall into place, like a jigsaw coming together. Even those who have never heard of the Mason Word, dream about this in metaphor. If you're not certain you're ready—me, I'm nowhere near ready—you should stay far away. To take away forever the hope of that one moment of understanding, this would be the worst kind of damnation."

And that was that. No Mason Word, perhaps. Let's go to the garden instead, for the rustling of the leaves in the warm sun sounds so pleasant.

But Oscar had been underground before. Everything, was it not? was a clue.

"This is the Marshmallow Exam," said Oscar.

"The what now?" said possibly everyone.

"It's just a trick," said Oscar. "Come back later when you're ready, only there is no later, or when you come back this place is a jungle of heating ducts and old pipes and everyone says, 'Mrs. Minge? We've never heard of Mrs. Minge.'"

"Oh, it's pronounced *ming-y*, dear. It's Scandinavian"

We've played fair with you, have we not, dear reader ? We roll up our sleeves before we pull out a card. We've kept nothing from you. You can close the book forever, if you wish. Has anything we've done taken this freedom away from you? *Possibly. Possibly.* But Oscar said, "I'm not falling for this. I'll take the Mason Word."

"You're crazy. This place is crazy," said Schwartz. "I'm not getting any dangerous words, whatever they are." But V.K. said,

"I'll go where you go, Oscar."

Mrs. Minge just pointed with one turquoise-clad arm (she probably also clucked her tongue). Straight, between two rows of columns, if that was something one could say. The breeze on

202

their faces blew from that direction, gusting at times as hand in hand the two walked forward, struggling, perhaps, into the harsher and harsher wind. The columns pulsed their pulses. The ceiling, if there was one, was invisible. No one had to say, *this is strange* or *I didn't see this coming*. Somewhere along the way their shoes had disappeared, and the floor—intricately tiled in byzantine and possibly Byzantine mosaic gold—was cold.

"I didn't see this coming," said Oscar unnecessarily.

Remember, I am not recording etc.

And in the end they came to a wall where a black curtain, worn and patched, covered a doorway. The wind from the doorway blew the curtain into whippings and snappings, like a locker-room towel. There were no columns here any more, and very little light. In the first edition of *Moby Dick* (1851), Ishmael dies, too, and no one survives to say call me anything. In the first draft of the first Conan the Barbarian story (1932), Cthulhu has a cameo.

"You're saying strange things," V.K. told Oscar.

"I didn't see this coming," said Oscar. "Are you sure you want to go in?"

"What would the Bollingen Prize judges say? 'I'm in for a penny...'"

"These are getting really obscure and difficult," Oscar said.

They cautiously, with some face slapping, slipped behind the curtain, and here was a small, still chamber, all made of stone, illuminated by torches hanging in brackets on the wall. The far side of the chamber was taken up by an enormous brazen head, or at least a brazen pan, the planes of its cheeks and forehead enormous and angular, emerging from the stone wall. Its mouth was on a hinge. Its great eyes stared blankly.

203

"Excuse me," said Oscar, his voice small in the stillness. "We're here about the Mason Word. They said it was cool. You can tell us."

The only preamble was a whirring and a creak, and the great jaw moved up and down as from deep within the brazen head's giant bellows-throat came the booming but clear word: "Green."

And then the brazen head intoned: "Churchmouse."

And then the brazen head intoned: "Ire."

And then the brazen head intoned: "Box."

And then all was still again.

"That was a good warm-up," said Oscar. "'Time is, time was.' But we're ready for the real deal, now." All was silent. "What's all this foolishness?" Oscar, the perishing, was about to add, but then he looked over at V.K.'s pan. It was illuminated, as from within, by a pharyngeal halo.

"Of course," said V.K., slowly, nodding, slowly.

"What's up?" asked Oscar.

But V.K. was laughing now, harder and harder. Maybe he gasped out: "The other side," but maybe that's silly, maybe he just gasped he was laughing so hard, holding his ribs together. He staggered a bit, and fell to one knee.

"Oh come *on*," said Oscar.

But they had to leave eventually, of course. They walked, with the morning-after shame-faced gawkiness Oscar had faked so many times in college, away from the head and the wind, more gentle at their backs, and through the forest of living columns. Mrs. Minge was visible in the far distance, chatting pleasantly with Schwartz, and all the world was filled with hope except for Oscar Cox. No man knew for certain he was the preterite except one man, and that man was he. No man knew for certain the

Mason Word would never be his except Oscar Cox.

"This is really awkward, and I'm so sorry," said V.K., when they were still some distance away.

"I know," said Oscar, who was already planning his next step. His next step was, of course, revenge. What had Oscar's whole life been but a secret revenge? You can't be a spoiler without being spoiled, but the whole world was full of people who had not been spoiled, and Oscar held their fate in his hands. If *They* did not know the Mason Words, *They* could hardly prevent him from typing them, emailing them everywhere. He could write a potboiler, a genuine thriller, and slip the Words in, pretending, perhaps that the reader had a choice of not reading them.

The way he'd been funneled into this one moment of despair seemed so improbable, so veiled in schemes and metaphors—doubtless Oscar was a catspaw all along. Doubtless he'd been chosen because revenge was his metier, revenge was his meat and drink. To be more specific: his meat was served cold; his drink was Amontillado. Who else could be counted on to spread the word, the Word, everywhere; whence *They* (with their presumable spiritual readiness) could glean it at their leisure.

V.K., meanwhile, continued: "It's just that I'm not going to be able to marry you."

"That's okay," Oscar found himself saying, mostly, as always, by instinct. "I think I'm going to become a celibate. Like a monk of sorts, or a Pythagorean. That'd be a fine thing to be, a Pythagorean."

And at that moment, he realized it was. It was a fine thing to be. It was a solution she should have hit upon long ago.

But there was an even better thing (Oscar was realizing) to be.

"Everything's very different," said V.K., "and I have a lot I have to do; but I do worry about you, Oscar."

"Don't worry, I'll be fine," said Oscar, who was not in fact lying. His voice sounded like it was breaking, heartbreaking, but actually it was pulsing with excitement. Cursed from the earth / punishment greater than I can bear. To be marked alone of all of humanity with the mark of Cain—surely we could do something with this material!

"You're not going to get revenge, are you?" V.K. asked.

The years would drag by, and the world would get weirder and worse. People would stop saying *me*, and then they would stop saying *them*. Politics would become television, which was unfortunate because television would be moribund and evil. Wars, already continual, would blossom into continuousness; the VFW, which for a century and a half had been a giant middle finger to Civil War vets, would become a giant middle finger to more and more vets. Everyone in America would believe two things simultaneously—1. that the police, when they arrived anywhere, inevitably shot an innocent person without provocation, and 2. that the police should be called for every contingency, such as a dog barking or a child on your lawn or a person of another race in your sight—and the cognitive dissonance required to believe both these numbers simultaneously would render the nation insane. Morgellons would be everywhere, and these would be the itchy years, the formicative years. Once again, everyone would be afraid of everything they had no reason to be afraid of, and they would forget to fear what they should. The best would lack all conviction etc. A fen of stagnant water etc. Graves, yes, but no glorious phantom bursting therefrom. You know the drill.

And of all the milling and teeming multitudes who toiled and wept their way through these days, very few had even seen the board on which they moved, hither and thither, like checkers. The alchemists and the tarotarians and the Neoplatonists and Susan Peters's badass-fujoshi underground army—perhaps a few of them saw the board, and some even plotted out their moves. How much rarer, like an early morning star, were those who suffered enlightenment: V.K. was one, and among the Elks and Rosicrucians there must have been others. "I have a lot to do," V.K. had said.

But there was only one Oscar. He alone was damned. Byron was dead and Melmoth was forgotten, but Oscar was damned. He was scarce able to afford suppression of the glee that kept threatening to burst out as a giggle. He alone was free. *Did you know that 666 divided by the Fahrenheit boiling point of water yields pi?* he thought but did not say. Perhaps tomorrow he would say it. Perhaps he would tell the Mason Word to the world; or perhaps he would pretend to, and remain unique. Regardless: He was free.

A tearing-up Oscar whispered, or perhaps lied: "Of course not," right into V.K.'s beautiful and literally beaming face.

About the Author

"I don't think Hal Johnson is a very unusual sort of a guy. He's just — well, the average American citizen and family man, the kind that are the backbone of the nation. I admire him and like him. I like his attitude. Until, that is, he gets behind the wheel of an automobile. At that point he changes. He changes from a careful, considerate citizen — to a menace."
  – "Driven to Kill," 1948 driver's safety film

Also by Hal Johnson:
  Immortal Lycanthropes
  Fearsome Creatures of the Lumberwoods
  The Big Book of Monsters
  Impossible Histories
  Apprentice Academy: Sorcerers
  Apprentice Academy: Knights

www.ingramcontent.com/pod-product-compliance
Lightning Source LLC
Chambersburg PA
CBHW061217170626
46809CB00007B/2513